P. S. Your Cat Is Dead

P. S. Your Cat Is Dead

JAMES KIRKWOOD

St. Martin's Griffin ✠ New York

www.stmartins.com

Library of Congress Cataloging-in-Publication Data

Kirkwood, James, 1930–1989.
    P.S. your cat is dead / James Kirkwood.—1st Griffin ed.
      p. cm.
    ISBN 0-312-32120-1
    1. Loss (Psychology)—Fiction. 2. Victims of crimes—Fiction. 3. New York (N.Y.)—Fiction. 4. Unemployed—Fiction. 5. Burglary—Fiction. 6. Black humor (Literature) gsafd I. Title.

PS3561.I72P15   2003
813'.54—dc21

                                                          2003047156

First published in the United States by Stein and Day, Inc.

First St. Martin's Griffin Edition: November 2003

10 9 8 7 6 5 4 3 2 1

For Arthur Beckenstein

Did things ever get so outlandishly rock-bottom rotten that you went around muttering, not necessarily out loud, but muttering nonetheless: *I don't believe it!* Then you might surprise yourself by a short, spastic burst of laughter, half expecting everyone to jump out shouting: "Surprise! Ah-hah, we had you fooled! *All* over!"

But they didn't and it wasn't. Wasn't over by a long shot.

For instance and to be blunt: if you were not successful at your profession (and had been trying your *ass* off), if you'd been robbed twice within three months, if your best friend had died and you were breaking up with your girl and your cat was sick and you got fired from a job, mightn't you start muttering: *I don't believe it!*

You'd try to keep your sense of perspective *and* humor, wouldn't you? You'd do your best to stave off thundering paranoia.

I tried.

But these, the above listed, they qualify more or less as major events. They stood up and spoke loudly for themselves. They *barked*.

It was the little things that indicated there might be a cosmic plot afoot.

The last time I went to the theater before the holidays had been with Kate. As we sat in the darkened orchestra minutes before the curtain went up, a loud sneeze broke the silence. It came from several rows behind us and it got a slight giggle. Kate and I had had several drinks and we were not fighting, so I was buoyed into a good mood. Without turning around I said in an audibly jovial voice: "God bless you!"

The sneezer, a woman, shouted back: "Oh, mind your own goddamn business!"

This earned a howl from the nearby rows of people. Kate laughed, so did I. But as the lights dimmed and the curtain rose and the play began, my disposition turned sour. I wanted to find that woman and punch her in her stuffed nose.

On the subway early in December, a crazy man—one of the army of sad crazy persons to be seen nowadays—teeth like Roquefort cheese, popeyed, balding, perhaps sixty-five, wearing three overcoats, and laden down with bags, papers, string-tied bundles, and one umbrella that had not survived a hurricane, took a seat across from me.

He was having a talk with God, rather *at* God, in a childlike, somewhat mincing voice that came from directly behind the bridge of his nose. "God! God!" he snorted. "God, you are a bad boy! Naughty God, *bad* God!"

I could not help grinning, out of nervousness, out of annoyance, that this crazy person had picked a seat directly opposite me. I was, also, not feeling in top shape. Kate and I had racked up a few nasty rounds that morning.

He went on. "Bad God, dirty God!" Despite what he was holding, his bundles and all, he managed to reach over and slap his *own* wrist. "Bad, bad, *dirty* God!"

The wrist slap did it. I smiled. In slapping his wrist he had dropped his umbrella. He snorted, reached down to retrieve it, then abruptly looked up and—caught my smile.

"Funny? *Funny?*" he demanded in his high nasal voice. He picked up the black and metal shredded mass that had been an umbrella and shook it at me. "You—you'll think it's funny when God takes a Fleet enema on *you!*"

He sputtered, settled back in his seat, then swiveled round to the man next to him. "He'll think it's funny when God takes a Fleet enema on *him!*"

I was close to extreme nervous laughter. The train slowed, I got up and quickly walked to the exit door, and when the train stopped and I was getting out—it was not my stop, I merely wanted to change cars—I could hear this poor deranged person shouting: "You'll think it's funny when God takes a Fleet enema on *you!*"

The phrase stayed with me.

At the time, I did not happen to know what a Fleet enema was. I did not know whether it meant a fleet enema, as in the Navy. I had a mental picture of the entire crew of an aircraft carrier lined up out on deck . . .

Or else it could be fleet, as in swift. He could have meant: God is going to take a very *quick* enema on you.

Whatever, during that dangerous week between Christmas and New Year's, that treacherous period so overburdened with memories of brighter better happier times, imaginings of what-should-be, what-might-have-been, of missing those relatives and friends who've died, or those lovers or friends who've parachuted from your life, or perhaps just drifted away hard on the heels of so many of your fondest dreams—during that week it became clear that someone, God or whoever, was taking an enema, Fleet or otherwise, and it had something to do with me.

There I sat, quietly, grimly, in total darkness, just sat there in the dark, in my old brown leather easy chair. Waiting. Waiting, but was the waiting—well, realistic? I was asking myself.

The phone rang again. Had been ringing off and on all afternoon. Without thinking, I grabbed the arms of the chair, swung forward and screamed across the room at it. "Shut up! Shut up! Shut up! Shut up! Shut up!" Really screamed, wrenching wartime, over-the-top, scare-the-achtungs-out-of-the-Nazis screaming.

The phone obliged. My throat hurt. Without thinking, I'd screamed, but *now* I thought, as I sat there suddenly aware of the unsteady heaving of my chest, the panting breaths. I thought: I am perhaps waiting for *two* things. I am first and foremost: waiting for the burglar to return. I knew he would; I was willing him back. The Return of the Burglar.

And, *oh, Jesus,* will he get a reception!

The other thing, this, somewhat spookier, had just seriously oc-curred to me. I might also be waiting to Join Aunt Jemima. Joining

Aunt Jemima was the euphemism my best friend Pete Williams had coined for flipping out. It translates easily enough: Aunt Jemima, pancakes, flipping.

Yes, it seriously occurred to me I might be extremely close to Joining Aunt Jemima! The little hairs scattered around at the top of my spinal column—Kate liked to tug on them; "Here, let me give you a comb-out," she'd say—stood up and touched my shirt in serious acknowledgment of this.

I kept sitting there in the dark. Maybe that was the unanswered phone call that would lure him back, as he'd been coaxed back two nights earlier. The phone had rung about eleven in the evening. I'd been in bed asleep and did not answer. Fifteen minutes or so later, after I'd gone back to sleep, I was awakened by footsteps coming up to the landing. Out of reflex, I switched the lights on from my bed. The footsteps quickly left. I cursed my reflexes. Oh, how I cursed them.

But I had not imagined I would be robbed *again*. I had been robbed twice that fall, once in September and then the final maddening ripoff in mid-November. Surely twice was a fair quota. By this time I'd had the door steel-backed, Fox-locked, etc. Yes, too late, I know, but still we do these things.

It had not occurred to me another attempt would be made—third time's a charm—but then two nights earlier the footsteps.

So there I sat in the dark—I'd even turned off the Christmas tree lights—waiting.

I moved my leg and kicked the looseleaf binder that contained my journal, not a serious journal, more of a day-by-day diary-journal. I rarely read back in it, except to look for the name of someone I'd met, or a date, or a record of when I'd done something.

This afternoon I had. I could not believe the grimness that had settled down like a great gray killer smog. I wanted to make sure I was not overreacting, so I read back, here and there, bits and pieces.

The documentation was present and accounted for. I could not believe it. I would alternate, sometimes the accent would be: I don't *believe* it, I don't *believe* it. Sometimes: I *don't,* I *don't* believe it.

I had also taken to saying out loud: "Add 'em up. Add 'em up, Bobby!" This, a recurrent line from the musical *Company.*

So while I'm sitting there on the afternoon of New Year's Eve day waiting for the burglar to return—and I guarantee you he will not disappoint either of us—I will tell you who this shaky person in the dark is.

The following sheet was put out by my agent.

James Zoole, 17 Cork Street, NYC Phone 243-4313 Service LE-2-1500

Age—32˙	Accents—English, French, Spanish˙˙˙
Height—6 ft.˙˙	Hobbies—swimming, tennis, skiing
Eyes—blue	Voice—light baritone
Hair—dark brown	Dance— soft shoe˙˙˙˙

· Although I was 38, I brought it down a few years. I rationalized it was because I *looked* younger, always played younger parts. This was true, but the prime reason was this: lopping off a few years gave me more time in which to succeed. At 32 if you have not become a household word, well, there's a bit of time. 38 is dangerously close to 40. If you haven't made it by 40—well, the reason for part of the shakes.

· · Actually 5 11½.

· · · I was once fired from dubbing a Japanese horror film for my lousy Japanese accent, so Japanese is not, over the objections of my agent, listed.

· · · · Barely.

BAD EGGS—featured, Broadway

A MAN FOR ALL SEASONS—Broadway

THE PLASTIC LOVE—featured, Broadway

BAREFOOT IN THE PARK—featured (replacement) Broadway

NEVER TOO LATE—(understudy for Orson Bean) Broadway

THE ANGELS OR WHOEVER—featured, off-B'way

THE STRONG SUIT OF THE LADY-BUG IS NOT FLYING—off-B'way

MY CERTAIN TOYS—starred, off-B'way

SOMETHING FOR NO ONE!—featured, off-B'way

JOAN OF LORRAINE—tour, Sylvia Sidney

CALL ME MADAM—summer tour with Martha Raye

CALL ME MADAM—summer tour with Elaine Stritch

WONDERFUL TOWN—Dallas, with Imogene Coca

PANAMA HATTIE—Dallas, with Vivian Blaine

WELCOME DARLINGS—tour with Tallulah Bankhead

WONDERFUL TOWN—N.Y. City Center, with Kaye Ballard

NEVER TOO LATE—featured, South African tour

MARY, MARY—summer tour opposite Kathryn Crosby

THE GLASS MENAGERIE—Ivanhoe Theatre, Chicago

BAREFOOT IN THE PARK—tour with Myrna Loy

COMPANY—bus and truck tour

TELEVISION

Four years featured part of Mickey Emerson on VALIANT LADY, CBS-TV.

GARRY MOORE SHOW	LOCK-UP
ED SULLIVAN SHOW	PERRY MASON
(sketch, Nancy Walker)	ODYSSEY
G.E. SUMMER THEATRE	LAWMAN
LAMP UNTO MY FEET	SHOTGUN SLADE
I SPY	STUDIO ONE

ALFRED HITCHCOCK PRESENTS	THE BIG VALLEY
KRAFT	LAW AND ORDER
DIVORCE COURT	TRUCK ROUTE
DAY IN COURT	VERDICT IS YOURS
NIGHT COURT	LOVE OF LIFE
COURT MARTIAL	LOVE IS A MANY
AS THE WORLD TURNS	SPLENDORED THING

COMMERCIALS: Coca-Cola, FAB, Ralston-Purina, Snow White, Breck Shampoo, Brite-Rite, Texaco, Tropicana Orange Juice.

INDUSTRIAL SHOWS: General Motors, N.A.M.S.B. (National Assoc. Men's Sportswear Buyers) (five seasons), Coca-Cola, Life, DuPont, Simco Products, Prudential Life, Norelco

OTHER: Dubbed films for TITRA, Army Training Films (7), Teenagers Unlimited, 26 weeks co-hosting with Lee Goodman, Mutual Network

STOCK COMPANIES: Lambertville, Oakdale, Newport, Westport, Kenley Players, Westport, Newport, Dennis, Skowhegan, Worcester, Bar Harbor, Neptune, Crag moor, Long Beach, Ivoryton, Guber-Ford-Gross circuit, Ogunquit, Buck's County, Pawtucket, North Shore Players, Grist Mill Playhouse, etc.

So this person sitting in the dark is/was an actor. But along about this time, if someone were to ask, "What do you do?" I would not proudly, as once I had done, announce, "I'm an actor." I would either have avoided a reply by sideswiping into another topic, or lied, or perhaps, according to my opinion of the questioner—prerequisites: honesty, sincerity, definitely no trace of smartass—I might have mumbled the truth, "I'm an actor."

Yet you might say from the list of credits, Well, now, that's quite a list, he's been busy as a switch engine, he *has* been working.

Yes, but have you ever heard of the name—James Zoole?

After twenty years in the business when your biggest credit is four years as "Son" of "Valiant Lady" on the now defunct television soap opera of that name, you— no, to put it more succinctly, if you've been an actor twenty years and have to be *asked* what it is you do—you have not got it made.

The phone rang again. I sat very still and counted the rings. One, two, three, four, five, six, seven, eight, nine, ten, eleven, twelve, thirteen, fourteen, fifteen, sixteen. Sixteen. Someone wants through. It could have been my only living relative, my Aunt Claire. It could have been Kate. It could have been my agent, Phyllis.

Or it could have been the Burglar.

After the phone stopped, I sat there for a while until I heard, in a loud voice: "Add 'em up. Add 'em up, Bobby!"

When you haven't planned to speak, when you haven't known you've spoken until you actually hear your very hollow voice, it can get to you.

As if to clear the air, I spoke again with full consent and knowledge. "Add 'em up. Add 'em up, Bobby!"

Herewith a few of the events I was adding.

ROBBERY I

My home was a fine oddball top-floor (third) loft-turned-apartment on Cork Street, a block-long cul-de-sac in the West Village, an easy dog walk from the Hudson River dock area. This apartment, inherited from an actor friend upon his marriage to an older and much wealthier lady two years previously, was a cocoon, an oasis of sanity in the midst of New York, a city for whom my love affair was on the serious wane.

One immense 40 x 36 room with brick walls and planked doors, plus a separate bathroom and two closets. The room was divided into three areas: a splendid kitchen with a free-standing butcher-block stainless-steel sink unit, built-in wall oven and cabinets; a sleeping area with a comfortable king-sized bed which could be screened off on two sides or not, as desired; and the main living area, sofa, easy chairs, rolltop desk, built-in bookshelves, stereo, and a working fireplace. Two small skylights, no more than two feet by two, broke up the expanse of the beamed ceiling, one over the bed, the other over the kitchen area.

The rent: $126.00. A steal at twice that.

On the evening of September 9, Kate and I returned to find the apartment thoroughly burglarized. The front wood door had been cut through, a hole punched out, and the lock slipped. The feelings upon being robbed I'd read about or heard from friends all applied. After the initial shock, a lockjaw rage at this invasion of privacy, more than distress at the loss of the articles in question: TV, stereo, typewriter, camera, a selection of clothes, cuff links, etc. A dirtying of my home, my *place*.

After the police had been called, had come and gone with such ill-concealed boredom that one almost felt like apologizing for having been robbed, Kate and I managed to squeeze a laugh out of it.

Pete Williams' wife had just that day given me a large bunch of fresh dill wrapped in white paper. I had placed it, still in its wrapping, in a large glass of water on the butcher block. Kate, who would put dill on ice cream she loved it so, noticed its absence. "Hmn," she said, "maybe we should find out what Julia Child was doing this evening."

Although insurance covered this first robbery, the investigator notified me I was hereby dropped—that year's policy was up in seventeen days—because the building was now a bad risk. The bakery on the ground floor had gone out of business, the aging hippie couple who made jewelry on the second floor had moved to New Mexico. The building had been sold and there was a rumor it was to be torn down. There was no one living there but me; if I were not home, a burglar could have a field day, he could hammer and saw to his heart's content, could even throw a hand grenade at my door and there would be no one to interfere.

Kate went shopping with me for replacements and my Aunt Claire sent a check which helped make up the difference between the current price of the items in question and what I received from the insurance company.

So I was robbed. Not too bad. Except for the nasty taste left by the experience itself. The apartment was no longer Safe Harbor; it had been violated. Whenever I went out I wondered if I would come home to find the door knocked in or ripped off. The hallways were eerie and not kept clean now that the building was empty except for me. Light bulbs by the stairs were not replaced unless I replaced them.

PETE WILLIAMS

Pete Williams was my closest and dearest friend. Bright, witty, talented, warm, feisty, and, even better, complex. He was rarely without surprise.

We met in 1966 when he directed the pilot for a proposed TV soap (that never got on) and we hit it off immediately. We began going out on double dates, later went to the same gym together, and soon we saw or talked to each other every day. He was engaged to a lovely girl, Didi Morrow.

One evening about three months into our friendship, after we'd taken our dates home, we stopped by a bar for a nightcap. We ended up having three or four and when we left and were walking down the street, Pete suddenly slipped his arm around my shoulder. He surprised me; there was extreme warmth and intimacy about the gesture. When I looked over at him, he grinned and said, "That bother you?"

"No . . ." I shrugged, trying to be as casual as possible. "Why?"

He shrugged in return, then gave my shoulder a squeeze. "Ever since I've known you, you got me pretending I don't have arms."

This stopped me dead. (That line stayed with me; it was typical of the way he put things.)

Pete stopped walking, too. He took his arm from around my shoulder and we stood there on the sidewalk facing each other as he dropped the zinger: "You know something, Jimmy? I'd like to go to bed with you."

The level offhand way in which he spoke let me know he was serious. So I said neither *What* nor *Come on* nor *You're kidding!*

I was, in fact, caught so completely off guard I was unable to speak. My expression must have said it all. The look on my face fractured him. He reared back, howling in laughter. This sudden explosion riled me, made me feel naïve and stupid. When he stopped laughing and saw that my confusion had turned to anger, he tapped me on the arm. Cocking his head, he said: "Listen, just because I'd like to make it with you doesn't mean I couldn't also beat the shit out of you. Kindly unglue the face."

When I told him I did not indulge, he merely shrugged and said, "Too bad, you don't know what you're missing." My face still had incredulity stamped all over it. "I know," Pete grinned, echoing my thoughts, "what about Didi? Oh, Jimmy . . ." He shook his head. "I can tell from your expression there's not much use talking about it. I love her, I adore her. I have, what shall I say, catholic tastes, I can't help it, so I enjoy them. The best of both worlds. Besides, if I didn't feel I had enough love in me for more than one person, I'd feel downright bankrupt!" Once again he looked at me and laughed.

We, of course, did talk about it. We talked about everything as our friendship deepened. He never made another overture. Oh, he kidded, but that was all.

I was best man at his wedding and am godfather to his son, Pete, Jr. His marriage to Didi was as successful and happy as any marriage

I've witnessed. This fall, after directing a soap for three years and several off-Broadway shows, he directed his first Broadway play, *Duet for Lemons*. A solid hit, still running. He had just signed for his first movie. He was on his way, moving up fast. No one deserved it more.

On October 16th, eleven days after the opening of his show, sitting in a movie house on Forty-second Street catching a double feature he'd missed—he died. Just died, sitting there alone in the balcony.

Pete Williams had recently turned thirty-seven, had no previous history of heart trouble, had rarely been ill.

His death was, to me, brutal, obscene, completely gratuitous. I did not take it well. By that, I mean I took it selfishly, as a deprivation, something taken away from me.

At the funeral parlor, when left alone with him—Didi had stepped outside with his mother—I stared and stared at that cocky upturned face, that nose, it was a pugnacious nose, the shock of chestnut hair, hair that seemed so alive now, the most alive part of him. I had belted down a few raw, burning shots, and suddenly I absolutely begged him: "Come on, Pete, come off it! Pete, that's enough, up and at 'em! Bad taste, Pete! *Pete*, joke over!"

I stopped and looked closely at him, stood there staring down at him. There, that mouth, the lips pressed together suppressing his grin, just a slight tug over in the corner, as if acknowledging the secret of his deception.

"Jesus, Pete—*come on now!*" And I caught myself with a hand raised. An impulse—to what! *Slap him?* Yes, actually slap him awake. Or make him flinch, scare him out of it by the threat of my gesture.

The next day, the day of the funeral, some minutes before those slick-haired carnationed monkeys in their foul gray suits closed that murderous gleaming mahogany lid for all time, I had an impulse to lean down and whisper: If you stop it—I'll make it with you. I will!

Pete's death still haunts me.

ROBBERY II

The second robbery was notable for the loss of one item.

I had, about ten months before, started work on a first novel. Although there was one very special story I felt I had within me to tell, that was not the primary reason for beginning to write.

I started to write because at the age of thirty-seven, which I was when I began, I felt all sense of dignity slipping away from my life. When you are diving into middle age—and it happens that fast, no getting back up on the board—and you cannot get up in the morning and, at the very least, put in a day's work at your profession, this is pitifully sad. Suffocation is what it is. I could not act unless what amounted to a committee composed of agent, producer, casting director, director, writer—and sometimes even a star or two—agreed that I was right for a part and, in effect, said: Yes, you may now be allowed to work for—what? Two days on a television show, or three weeks in an industrial, or two weeks in stock. Or half a day on a voice-over commercial.

My hand was constantly extended, in full stretch asking for work. I was beginning to feel the cramp. Even when I *was* working, there was the certainty that in two days or five weeks I would go begging again. I would be back in that depressing unemployment line, the one that ended at a fat Puerto Rican lady whose face tightened when she looked at my card, as if the word "actor" read "shit."

When Kate, who was a successful fashion photographer, one of the few women in the business, got up in the morning to go off to work, I would often fix her juice and coffee as she hurriedly pulled herself together. She would peck me goodbye at the door and I would be left there in my bathrobe on the cozy end of a domestic scene. I would cringe when she would sometimes say, "Jim, you don't have to get up, go back to sleep for a while."

All too true, there was nothing to get up for. I could as well spend my time sleeping as sitting there awake waiting for my agent to phone with an appointment to read for a commercial, along with perhaps fifty other actors, vaguely my height, weight, and age. Often so many actors showed for one part, you knew whoever was doing the picking must be punchy from the pure swarming mass of them, all with charm stops pulled to out. It amounted to Russian roulette.

Even worse, there were many days when the phone didn't ring.

This next part of the problem is so basic one needn't even have heard of Dr. Freud. Lately, I was finding that the frequency and quality of erection diminished in proportion to the number of days out of work.

Bad deal. Not only for me but for Kate.

A good night's sleep was getting hard to come by. One night I awakened at three in the morning, cold and sweaty, clutched by a prickly fear that the job I'd finished twelve days before was undoubtedly the last I'd ever get my hands on. I made a pot of coffee, took a shower, cleaned off my desk, got out a lined legal pad, and actually wrote the first nine pages of my novel by the time eight o'clock rolled around.

The relief! The joy to get up in the morning and have something to do, something I *could* do without awaiting results from the Central Committee.

I worked slowly if not steadily. Because I did, of course, get other acting jobs, and then there are the appointments, the auditions, the singing lessons, the readings that take up so much of an actor's time. Pete's death put a stop to all activities for over six weeks. I would just stare at the page and think of Pete, sometimes even write down his name. And mutter to God, then curse him, then stop talking to him altogether. But—write, no.

Now the perverse part. Kate is an extremely inquisitive girl. I would not talk about the book, let alone allow her to read my scribblings. The story was my secret, the more I kept it to myself, the stronger the compulsion to write it down. A good feeling.

One night when Kate was high and happy, she mentioned to mutual friends that I was, in fact, working on a novel. "Oh, really?" "True, Jimmy?" "How great!" "What's it about?"

"Oh, he won't talk about it, can't get a word out of him," Kate said. "But it's good," she added, beaming a wide smile.

The way in which she said it, the way it slipped out, together with her smugly satisfied smile, made me suspicious. "How do you know?" I asked.

She made a bad attempt at quick recovery. "I mean," she said, "I just know it is. I know you can write."

"You've been peeking!"

Immediate anger. "I have not been—*peeking!* I haven't! How dare you—" But her reddened face announced she had.

We had a dandy argument, during which I accused and reaccused her of looking into the desk drawer where I kept the pages. Infuriated and still denying, she snorted: "If you're so nervous, if you're so untrusting, buy a safe and keep your goddamn book in *there*. No, *I'll* buy you a safe!"

She didn't buy a safe, I didn't either. I did buy a small metal cabinet with a locked drawer and after that I kept the pages in there.

On November 14th, two days after I'd haltingly started back to work on the book, I came home to find my cat, Bobby Seale, in the downstairs hall of the building. I picked him up, climbed the stairs, and found the door pried off its hinges. Not only had the *new* television set and stereo been taken but the metal cabinet was gone.

The metal cabinet, by this time, contained nothing but my passport, a set of twelve dirty pictures Pete had given me, and two hundred and twelve pages of my novel. The only copy of the two hundred and twelve pages.

It is hard to describe my emotions. Anger? Rage? No, more like apoplexy.

Or insanity.

For the first week or ten days I harbored, sloshing around inside the mess that was me, the shaky hope/prayer that the burglar, once he'd discovered the total uselessness of the contents of the metal cabinet, might somehow return my book to me.

As the days passed it was apparent the book had been simply thrown out with someone's trash or left lying in an alley to be rained upon and blown away.

I was victim, not of burglary, but of kidnaping. My child had been taken away and destroyed.

The fantasies I had of catching the unspeakable bastard would fill a twelve-volume set of Gothic horrors. Oh, the scenes of torture, of bloodletting, that crammed my head, awake and dreaming.

This latest misfortune hit hard. I was inconsolable and miserable to be with. Miserable to be with myself, and miserable to be with Kate.

She was not really devious; she was curious and high-spirited and she'd finally admitted reading approximately one chapter. She loved it, she said she also promised she would not attempt to read more until I made an offer. Still, I had bought the metal cabinet. The pages had merely rested in my desk drawer, undisturbed, during the first robbery. But now that she'd forced me to keep them locked up, well, naturally Kate came in for her share of the blame.

I blamed myself, too. I even blamed my cat, Bobby Seale, whom I loved, berated him for sitting idly by while the burglar made off with my book.

"Can't you attack! Are the claws only for the furniture? Jesus, I ought to trade you in for a police dog, you rotten no-good black bastard, you!"

COMPENSATION?

A few days after that, I received notice of eviction in the mail. I expected it, it figured, I shrugged. I was still numb from the loss of the book and not feeling any too happy about the apartment along about this time anyhow. Still, Kate persuaded me to contact a lawyer, Mr. Weisscoff, who assured me I would be able to remain in the building another six months at least. He made me promise not to talk to the new landlords or their lawyers, to refer everything to him. He assured me we could eventually expect a cash settlement if I did not panic.

Then, as I was feeling this was the most outrageous, the longest-lasting, record-holding, prize-winning enema of all time—there came a consolation prize.

Two weeks after the second robbery my agent sent me to read for a play, *Married Alive*, to star the current generation's answer to Debbie Reynolds, Miss Bebe Peach. I read three times in five days and to my surprise ended up with one of the three leading male roles, that of Tommy. I was to get featured billing, $450 a week, and rehearsals were to start January 2nd.

I knew that eventually I would get around to redoing the book. It would be hard, harder to try to re-create what I'd written than creating it in the first place. It was too soon to launch back into it, but I knew I would.

Kate and I celebrated that Friday night. We painted the town, used up all the primary colors, then stayed in bed almost all weekend. I was extremely virile.

KATE

This did not mean things were fine between Kate and me. We were undoubtedly at the end of our year-and-five-month affair, but no one knew how to yell "Uncle!"

There were many strikes against us. Kate made more money than I did, she was more extravagant, more open, more adventurous, more opinionated, more—almost more than I could handle. In every way except one.

I had known her slightly, had seen her around at parties for almost two years. She had enormous green eyes, sea-green eyes, which slayed me, rich sable-brown hair worn in a ponytail, which also slayed me, long lovely legs, a tiny waist, flat stomach, and just-right medium-sized breasts that one could never imagine falling. Her personality, opinions, style, her entire approach to life, were so strong, so head-on, I had no doubt she was a man-eater. I was as intimidated by her as I was attracted to her.

I knew she noticed me; every so often at a gathering those green eyes would fasten on me. Frankly, I interpreted her look as a musing appraisal over whether my private parts might be worthy enough to be added to her collection.

One night at a party given by our mutual friend, Nettie Madden, I got quite drunk and became increasingly sullen over my apprehension of her. I brooded, keeping an eye on her. She was bowling over a small group of people with her personality. She had just told a joke or story and as I passed behind her chair on the way to the bar, she tossed her head back, laughing her infectious laugh. I looked down into her green eyes, suddenly stopped, grabbed her ponytail, pulled her head back, and planted an upsidedown kiss squarely on her lips.

She returned the kiss with her usual aplomb, as if it had been rehearsed, then said: "Hmn, don't leave without checking with me." As I made my way to the bar, stunned by my behavior, I heard her say, "I hope he hasn't started something he doesn't intend to finish."

I didn't intend to, not at all. I waited a decent interval, said good night to Nettie, and as I walked toward the front door I heard Kate's voice: "Say there, *Tarzan*? Swinging off by yourself?"

I turned around as her group laughed. "No," I lied.

"Oh?" she laughed. "I see, you were going to wait for me *downstairs*. Right?"

Another laugh; I was furious. "Yes," I said in the strongest steadiest voice I could muster. "With a club!"

The laugh topped hers. Kate got up without further ado. "Good night all," she said to her group. "Nettie, good night, I had a lovely time." The next thing we were riding down in silence in the elevator, then we were in a cab on the way to her apartment. Not a word was spoken. I was seized by bedroom fright. I kicked myself for kissing her, for starting it. When the cab pulled up to her apartment on East Fifty-sixth Street, she merely said, "Nightcap?"

"Sure." There was no decent way out, although my brain was scrambling for some honorable way to avoid direct confrontation with this highly veneered, entirely shellacked manikin.

Up in the elevator, keys out of the handbag, door open. As she stepped onto the polished wood floor of her living room her feet flew out from under her and she took what she later described as "a good klutzy hard fall." There she lay on her back, the veneer gone, shellac cracked. She looked helpless and dear. "Blew it," she said. She began to laugh; so did I. Soon I was on the floor with her and we began our lovemaking right there.

By the time we finally reached the bed and I was poised naked and extremely ready above her, she said, in a small little-girl voice: "Be gentle, don't hurt me!"

Don't hurt me! That from her. Her plea made me so happy I could only grin my head off. And perform beautifully.

She was completely feminine, soft and vulnerable in bed. That, I might add, was about the only place she was. I loved the glazed, almost frightened look of wonder as she neared orgasm. I loved her in bed. Sexually we were perfectly matched. No need ever to discuss timing, rhythm, position, or any part of making love. Once we started, it always happened together. *Always.* And always she allowed me to be the instigator and the leader. Right or women's liberation wrong, she was wise in bed. She knew how to get the best from her man. Sex was our mutual safe ground, our meeting place.

Of course, there is that six months' grace period of discovery before each other's idiosyncrasies begin multiplying in number and annoyance like loaves and fishes, the period during which you tell each other all that went before, made up of truth and part-truth, mixed with imagination, wishful thinking, and fascinating storytelling. That period had ended.

In public and out socially, Kate often acted like Rosalind Russell playing Bella Abzug. This I found annoying. She would not hesitate to call out in a restaurant, "Say, Wally Waiter, what do you call *this*?" as she shoved a dish not to her liking at the man. "Take this back to Charlie Chef and tell him medium rare does not mean cremated!"

That kind of behavior. With waiters, cab drivers, salesmen, etc.

One day I made up a list in my journal of things I liked about Kate and those I didn't. Lovemaking topped it off, as indicated. Then: I admired her looks, style, impulsiveness, generosity, enthusiasm, candor, and humor. I did not admire her rudeness, her opinionated statements on almost any subject without much thought or real intelligence to back them up; Kate was bright and quick but not overly intelligent. Although she was personally immaculate, she could turn a kitchen or bathroom into a health menace in a matter of minutes. At times she lacked a certain compassion for her fellow man. She was also intolerant of the faults of others.

Mine, for instance.

I could also have made up a list of what Kate did not like about me. She did not like or respect my profession, or my approach to it, she did not approve of my caution and conservatism in most things: money, clothes, social behavior. She disliked the name "Jimmy," preferring to call me Jim. "It's time you stopped being the fuzzy boyish type—cute as you are—and started playing leads." (I like Jim myself, but most people called me Jimmy.) She hated my cat.

But soon she will make an appearance and speak for herself. So enough. Except for one last item, almost the clincher, of which she disapproved: Claire Hubbard, my aunt.

Before the burglar appears, a few words about Claire.

And the last of the Fleet enema.

CLAIRE

My mother's sister, Claire, was married at nineteen to Earl Hubbard, who left her eleven months later. My mother's husband, my father, left *her* when I was five and returned to England. My mother got over it, going on to other marriages, but Claire did not. She retracted into a tight knot of spinsterhood.

She worked herself up to executive secretary, worked hard and made good money, money she spent on the protracted illnesses of both of her parents, my grandparents; both had strokes and lingered for years. She also helped support, off and on, my mother, a beautiful tender lost alcoholic with a magnetic drive toward men who would mistreat her on a grand scale, until her death from cirrhosis of the liver seven years ago. Claire also helped put me through two years of college until the deadly acting virus struck, a terminal virus, that.

Claire tended to her obligations, she came through as self-appointed head of the family. One heard about her sacrifices but then they were certifiable, she made them.

For seventeen years Claire was executive secretary to Henry Graebner, real estate developer, stockbroker, and general financier, a man I never liked, one whose basic reactionary meanness stuck out like so many warts. But he was shrewd, he did well. In 1965 he and his equally nasty wife divorced; it was a messy suit. Claire stuck by him, admired him, was his strong right arm.

Claire. If you can imagine Gloria Swanson playing an executive secretary, that might give you a clue, the tightness around the mouth, the smile, dazzling, but again, tight and quick to snap shut once it had done its duty. The eyes narrowing, not sensually but in appraisal and often in disapproval.

I appreciated Claire more than I loved her. I was won over by her liking of me, by her feeling of family toward me. I was also saddened by her basic loneliness. But most of all, I appreciated what she'd done for her parents, my mother, and me. And for what we'd been through together.

Henry Graebner died of a massive coronary in 1968. To spite his ex-wife and his three children, whom he disliked and had provided for with modest trust funds, he left Claire eight hundred thousand after taxes and his house in Riverdale. The will was contested and Claire was dragged into court. There were unpleasant accusations, but the will was upheld. I know Claire was not his mistress. She could not stand to be touched, let alone entered.

There's no denying I was delighted to have a wealthy relative, the only one on the horizon, wealthy or not. There was a three- or four-month period of celebration. When Claire had only her salary and a few small investments, she had always been generous, but when she stopped working and moved to the house in Riverdale, it appeared she had inherited not only Graebner's money but also many of his attitudes. Always slightly cool to the world, she became downright chilly, suspicious, and began using her money as a tool to get people to do what she supposed was best. Claire had never been a liberal, but now she was headed in her thinking back to the Dark Ages. Money made her not a nicer person, not at all.

She was now acting the part of a rich woman. If you could imagine Gloria Swanson playing an executive secretary, now imagine an executive secretary trying to play Gloria Swanson. Worse, much worse.

Now, however, comes the dirty part. It comes out in a scene with Kate on the way home from Riverdale Christmas Eve, a Christmas Eve made totally unpleasant by Kate's open hostility toward Claire. Although their loathing was mutual, Claire, being more devious, masked hers somewhat.

Kate and I had exchanged our presents earlier at my place. That part of the evening was fine. But once we arrived at Riverdale for dinner with Claire and a few of her charity cases, the evening turned to disaster.

Kate slugged them down until she was quite drunk. When I opened an envelope containing a check for five hundred dollars, my Christmas present from Claire, Kate muttered, "What's the penalty for blackmail in New York State?" When Claire said she hoped the play would be a hit, then added it didn't really matter because "Jimmy knows he's got me and when I die . . ." Kate sang the first few bars of "Promises, Promises." It was that kind of outrageous behavior. Open warfare.

We finally made a bumpy departure and drove down the parkway in Kate's car in a frozen Christmas Eve silence until we got to the toll just before the West Side Highway. I could tell Kate was close to exploding; finally it bubbled up out of her.

"Oh, God, Jim, I can't *stand* it! And New Year's, you promised to go to her party *New Year's*. Well, I refuse to see her again, you can goddamn well go without me!"

"I said I'd just stop by for a while, she's going away the next day."

"Thank Christ. Can't you see what she's doing to—"

"Kate, let's leave it. You were rude, you messed up the entire evening, I don't want to talk about it."

"*I do want to talk about it!*" This, spoken like Napoleon.

"Kate, whatever you say, she's my aunt and—"

"She's a cunt!" Kate shouted. "An old dried-up—"

"Jesus, Kate, I can't stand it when you use that word, I really can't!"

"And I can't stand seeing you blackmailed!"

"Blackmailed!" A snort from me.

"Yes, blackmailed in the nastiest possible way. You would never put up with her, with the things she says, with what she stands for, if it weren't for the promise of inheriting her money! I feel absolutely dirty after spending an hour with the two of you." She looked out the window to her right. "I feel like jumping in the Hudson for a good clean bath, and we all know how dirty *it* is!"

"Shall I stop the car?"

She slapped me. I jammed on the brakes, swerving over to the side. When I'd taken my hands off the wheel I reached over and slapped her. She was expecting it, she'd shielded herself, so it was not a satisfying slap. Still she screamed and got out of the car. "Exactly, and you feel dirty, too, which is precisely why you slapped me!"

I got out, ran around, and grabbed her. "What did you expect me to do, keep on driving into town with you belting me in the face?" I was shaking with anger and not because she'd slapped me. She was right. I did feel dirty. But I would not then own up to it, barely to myself and certainly not to her.

A car slowed down at the sight of us, obviously in positions of distress at the side of the highway. "Get in!" When she hesitated, I grabbed her again. "Get in, goddamnit!" I shoved her toward the car.

"Oh, big man! Not such a big man with her, listening to all that tight-assed bigotry, swallowing what pride you have. It's sickening." When we were under way again, she continued her filibuster. "And don't tell me about all her good deeds, she wears them around her neck like rocks. Your mother was her *sister*, that's why she took care of her. So she helped you through two years of college. Take a bank loan and pay her back!" Now she mimicked Claire. " 'Jimmy doesn't have to worry because when I die . . .' Jesus, the Aunt Claire Doll, wind it up and it promises to die! She's just the type to keep you on the hook until she's ninety-eight and then leave it all to a hospital for unwed canaries! If she really wanted to help, why doesn't she do it now, while she's alive, give you ten thousand and say, here, relax, but no, she's—"

I slammed on the brakes, pulling the car over to the side again. "Jesus H. Christ I am sick of you and your endless talk!" Her eyes were wide, she looked momentarily frightened—I noted with something approaching joy. "Just for Christmas, could you suspend, a cease fire, a cease yammering, could we just have a little silent goddamn fucking *night*! Could we! *Could we!*" I was shouting, I'd surprised her into silence.

I started up and we drove on without talking. The freeze was on. When we approached the Fifty-seventh Street exit, Kate said, "Get off here, I'll stay at my place."

"Thank Christ!"

Kate was going to Pennsylvania to spend Christmas day and the next with her father and stepmother. It was agreed I would stay in town and read over the play, work on my part. We were planning to spend the next few days and New Year's Eve together before the start of rehearsals. I stopped the car at Seventh Avenue. "I'll get out here. It's been a *fun* Christmas."

"Thanks to that bitch! We couldn't spend it together, you had to drag me up there, didn't you? Goddamn me for going!"

"Yes, goddamn you!"

"Look, Jim, this is ridiculous. We're all out of—You promised to stop by Claire's, don't deny yourself! Spend the whole New Year's with her. Count me out. I refuse to see her again, there's no point.

We'll check each other after the holidays and see if it's worth picking up the pieces."

"If that's the way you feel."

"That's the way I feel."

The next morning, Christmas day, I phoned Kate but she'd already gone, or else chose not to answer. In the afternoon I went to have Christmas dinner with Pete's widow, Didi, Pete Jr., and Didi's mother. We put up brave fronts but no matter what we did, it was a bust. If we talked about Pete, the very air we breathed between words seemed to choke us. If we avoided talking about him, it was all too obvious *what* we were avoiding. Pete Jr. was a carbon copy in miniature of his father. At the table, when he sighed and slapped his hand to his forehead in a mugging take, Didi said, "God, so much of Petey in there. Sometimes I feel it's the Incredible Shrinking Man."

The truth was, we missed him so very much that just being together constituted a memorial service. Not good.

When I left around five in the afternoon, Didi kissed me good-bye. "Jimmy . . ." She glanced down, then back up at me. I knew what she was going to say. "Let's take a breather for a while. Don't you think?"

"Yes. I love you."

"I—too do you . . ." she sputtered, then quickly closed the door.

Bobby Seale did not eat his supper that night. On nights that Kate and I were not together, he slept with me. I liked the feel of his lumpy warmth next to me. This night when I put him on the bed, thereby letting him know it was all right, he thumped down, slunk into the bathroom, and flopped on the tile floor. I was lonesome, feeling miserable. I retrieved him, put him back on the bed. Once more he jumped off and sought the bathroom floor. "No-good black bastard! You really pick your time, don't you?"

He was still on the bathroom floor in the morning. The whir of the electric can opener always sent him trotting to bump my leg. Nothing. I opened his favorite, tuna with egg, even brought it to him. A perfunctory sniff, that was all. I felt his nose, it was hot. I felt my nose, it was hot, too. I wondered if all that was nonsense.

I read through the script, missed Kate, missed the warmth of her in bed more than I missed sitting across from her in a restaurant or being with her at a party, but miss her I did. I began to get nervous tremors about the approaching first day of rehearsal.

That day, December 26, I did not go out, except briefly to the store. I was hoping Kate might call from Pennsylvania. Bobby Seale refused dinner. Nose still hot, listless.

No call from Kate.

First thing next morning I took Bobby Seale to the vet's. He looked so helpless lying there on a miniature operating table with a thermometer stuck up him. So sick he did not even resist this indignity. He was running a high temperature; tests would be made and the vet told me to call back in the evening.

When I got back to the apartment I broke down and phoned Kate at her office. Her voice was crisp as she told me she was leaving early afternoon on a rush assignment for two days' shooting in San Juan.

"Oh, I'm sorry." Silence. Go ahead, *say it.* "I missed you. I was hoping we could—"

"Jim, I'm in an awful rush."

"I have nothing to do, could I drive you out to the airport?"

"Too complicated, I have three models on my hands, plus my assistant and the account man. We're going in a limo."

"Oh . . ."

"We'll talk when I get back." Then, to someone else, "No, not those, the ones in the large manila envelope. Yes. No, *under* those!"

Couldn't she even finish a brief conversation with me? Still, I made an offering. "I'm sorry about Christmas Eve."

"Me too."

Silence again. Oh? *That* sorry? She was speaking in shorthand.

"About New Year's—"

Her snap again. "I told you, forget about me, I want no part of her, wasn't I clear enough?"

I'd been about to say I'd stop by Claire's early for a brief visit, then meet Kate and we'd spend it together. Her attitude was such that I merely said: "Yes, I was just going to wish you a Happy New Year."

"Same to you. We'll talk."

"I can't *wait*! Goodbye."

"Goodbye."

I was shaking when I hung up. It occurred to me she was actually about to end it—and didn't much care. How childish we are. I was. Immediately I thought: No, if it's to be ended, *let me.*

That afternoon the vet informed me Bobby Seale had a serious kidney infection. He assured me he was being given the best possible care and would pull through, but he was one sick cat. Poor Bobby Seale. I realized even more, without his purring blackness, without all the leg bumpings and games of hide-and-seek and surprise attacks, what good company he was. I had never liked cats, but I loved this mongrel.

When I'd first taken over the apartment I'd made his acquaintance up on the roof. He was a real young tom, a renegade, and wary of humans. If the roof door was left open, he would sometimes come down to investigate the hallway in his search for food. I began leaving milk and tidbits up on the roof for him. Our friendship soon blossomed. One night I heard distant plaintive crying. I went up to the roof and found him, bloody and beaten, an ear torn, whole patches of fur missing, a leg badly injured. He just lay there, thoroughly whipped. "Poor bastard!" I picked him up, brought him down to my apartment, and nursed him back to health. He never left.

The next day, December 28, I spent cleaning the apartment, taking out laundry and dry cleaning, doing all the chores I wouldn't be able to do once rehearsals started. Claire called and in one of her sly ploys, to make sure I'd show up New Year's, asked me to pick up some paper hats, noisemakers, and the like. I shopped for those and bought several bottles of champagne, too. Just in case Kate . . .

I switched to thoughts of the play. It was by far the healthiest item to concentrate upon. Rehearsals were only days away; there is something wildly exciting about a company assembling for the first time on stage. There is also something strangely sexy about it. I can't pin it down, there just is.

The morning of December 29 I worked on the script, paid a few bills, changed a light bulb in the hall. Getting ready for the big push.

In the afternoon I went uptown, deposited Claire's Christmas check, and bought a new pair of slacks and a double-knit dark-blue blazer for rehearsals. The purchase made me feel good. I thought of going to a movie but just on chance I phoned my message service. Kate might have gotten back and . . .

"Please call your agent."

Her office was only a few blocks away so I decided to stop by. I walked briskly over to Sixth Avenue; I'd pumped myself into a good mood. I was relieved this messy holiday season was almost over. Soon I'd be in rehearsal, back to life as I liked it best—working.

The look on Phyllis's face froze my blood. She was a pretty woman in her fifties, unusually feminine for an agent, with something of the mellowness of Simone Signoret about her. Today her face was granite as she rose to kiss me on the cheek and asked me to sit down.

"Something's wrong," I said.

"I don't want to beat around the bush, Jimmy. You're out of the play."

My heart dropped twenty-eight floors to the lobby and shattered. Phyllis handed me an envelope. I opened it with difficulty. The numbness with which her words struck me had already extended to my fingers. A check made out to me for nine hundred dollars.

"Two weeks' salary. They didn't have to, they felt so bad, the producers and the director—not as bad as you feel, I know. Oh, Jimmy—how I dreaded this!"

There was nothing to say. I had no voice or appetite to speak even if there had been.

"Want to know why?" I nodded. Now she smiled, for one unbelievable moment I thought she might break into laughter. "It's a heartwarming Broadway story. Bebe Peach is engaged to a young Hollywood actor, Kenneth Walt—done a few things lately. He signed for a film to be directed in Spain by Peter Holmes, now *Sir* Peter Holmes. On the third day of shooting Sir Peter and Kenneth Walt had an argument about a piece of business. On the set in front of the entire cast and crew, Kenneth Walt called Sir Peter, excuse the language, 'a dizzy cunt.' Sir Peter said, 'I beg your pardon!' and Kenneth did him the favor of repeating the phrase. Kenneth Walt was sent packing.

"Bebe Peach contacted the producers, insisted he play your part. Impossible, they said, the part was cast, contract signed, impossible. She threatened to pull out unless they took him. They've been with lawyers since the day before Christmas. Seems she'd had a bad back for years and can get a doctor's certificate. There's nothing they could do, their hands were tied. So, Jimmy, my dear, there you have it. Dizzy C in Spain and you're out here."

Now I spoke: "I don't believe it."

There will be no description of that evening's binge, the majority of which I don't recall anyhow, except to say it was a Rip-Roaring, All-Stops-Out, Holy Pisser worthy of Brendan Behan and Dylan Thomas combined. It ended up in disgust and vomit and I consider myself lucky that I made it home. I don't remember how I got back but I remember waking up there, vomiting more, and spending the entire day in bed in the company of a hangover that was in such possession of me, bound my head so tightly, clutched my stomach so strongly and trembled my hands with such force that it was tangible. I could speak to it and did: "Jesus, let go, give up, I'll pay you, I'll sell my soul, let go, please, dear God!"

I took aspirin, Alka-Seltzer, Pepto-Bismol. By evening my hollow stomach craved food, demanded it. I threw on old clothes and shook my way to the delicatessen. When I got home I ate a large can of tunafish saturated with mayonnaise, egg rolls, a small barbecued chicken, a container of cole slaw, a shrimp cocktail and a quart of chocolate-chip-mint ice cream.

Bloated and pokey, I went back to bed and fell asleep. The phone rang. I glanced at the clock: eleven fifteen. But as I had stopped speaking to the world I did not answer. I drifted back to not such a sound sleep. A while later footsteps and the creaking of the stairs awakened me. Without thinking I switched on the lights. The footsteps quickly descended the stairs.

This is where you came in.

The effrontery of the burglar, a burglar, any burglar, coming back now, at such a time, so enraged me that the entire next day I sat in the apartment, waiting. Waiting and waiting.

I was in full siege. Now the cumulative events of the fall, ending up with—what?—*dizzy cunt*—what a dirty gratuitous joke! Even more perverse because it is an unfavorite word of mine. Then again, Kate's use of it, Somehow it all tied together in a macabre scheme.

Though I could not, in my present maddened condition, put it all together, it was all there, no doubt of that.

If only, *if only I had my book* I could creep off to Siberia or North Dakota, resign from life, and write it! But even that—

I don't believe it!

Another phrase of Pete's came back to me. When disasters multiplied, he would say, half jokingly: "Don't taunt the wretched!"

But *really* don't taunt them!

Hair of the dog and to keep me company I made a drink. It was in the late afternoon that I got up to go to the bathroom and caught sight of my face in the mirror. I was surprised at the pair of crazy red-rimmed eyes that burned back at me. I laughed, I was so surprised. I hadn't shaved in two days and I was looking hung over, scraped out, and ratty. I looked very unlike my real self, looked like someone who'd put in time in a foxhole. Right, I was in siege. I wanted confrontation with the enemy. I shouted in the mirror: "Come and get me, come on, come and get me!"

I laughed again and muttered: "Jesus, what am I shouting at *myself* for?"

The phone rang, perhaps the fifth or sixth time it had rung that day. "Shhh . . ." I said. I walked quietly back to the darkened living room. The phone rang twelve times. It occurred to me, only then, to disengage the Fox police bar so the burglar would only have to slip the lock on the door. Surely he could do that.

I sat back down holding the metal bar across my lap. That would be a good weapon to bash his head in with. The phone rang twice again. The sky outside the windows was a leaden dark gray. Soon it began to snow, heavy thick flakes falling straight down. I watched, allowing myself to be hypnotized by them. As I sat there trying to hear the *sound* of their falling, I heard another sound, faint at first, but unmistakable. Footsteps. In the downstairs hall.

Quickly I got up and crept to the door. I noticed only then that I had no shoes on, only socks. My heartbeat tripled, at least, and I was grinning, could feel the grin stretch my mouth. I would stand there in silence and darkness and wait until he'd used his ingenuity to break in—then he would meet *my* ingenuity.

How slowly the footsteps came up to the third floor, how cautious he was! I felt such a thrill. I trembled out of excitement, not out of fear.

The phone rang. My immediate response was to "Shhh" it, but no, perfect, let it ring, let him hear it *not* being answered. It only rang six times before stopping. By that time his footsteps had reached the door, I could tell. I could sense him right there, inches away.

Silence, then a knock, a pause, then three knocks. And my name. "Zoole?" I didn't answer. "Telegram for Zoole." The voice was unmistakably that of an old man.

I turned the lock and yanked the door open. The man, old, overcoated, and knit-capped, jumped back and put a mittened hand to his chest. "Oh, oh," he gasped. "I didn't hear you. You—you—took me by surprise." He smiled a tiny frightened smile. "Mr. Zoole?"

"Yes."

"Telegram, sign here." He fumbled for a small yellow slip and a small yellow pencil. When I'd signed and he'd handed me the telegram, he said, "Happy New Year."

"New Year?"

"Yes, have a Happy New Year. Careful if you go out, it's getting slippery."

I'd forgotten it was New Year's Eve. I gave him a dollar bill, he thanked me warmly and left.

The telegram was from Claire. "Trying to phone you for days. Expecting you to help out at party tonight. Know you won't let me down. Love, Claire."

"Shit, shit, shit!"

Oh? Do you feel tricked that it wasn't the burglar? How do you think I felt? Standing there with only a telegram in my hand. A telegram from Claire.

Even so, my obsessive belief that he would appear was not shaken. Not a bit.

So it was New Year's Eve. To my one track-mind, this spelled lucky. A burglar could make a walloping night of it New Year's. No one was paying attention New Year's. I would be paying attention.

The stores would be closed soon and I had to lay in supplies. Also, I wondered whether I shouldn't buy a gun. If the burglar had one, or even a knife, I would be no match for him with my steel bar. I put on shoes and an overcoat, placed the Fox bar on, and double-locked the door. I wanted to take no chances while I was out for half an hour at most.

The snow was indeed slippery, but there was no wind and it was not particularly cold. I decided to concentrate first on the purchase of a gun and hurried over to Waverly Place. Christ, where did one get a gun? So much talk about anyone being able to buy a gun anywhere and I could not for the life of me think where to get one, except at a sporting goods store and that would be uptown. At Sixth Avenue, standing there in the snow, looking up and down and all around, slightly dazed, I heard my name.

"Jimmy! Jimmy Zoole!"

It was Carmine Rivera, a stage manager I'd worked with Off-Broadway. He was the only certified, self-publicized sex maniac I knew; his nickname was C. C. for Crazy Carmine. He'd often tried to get me involved in his fun and games. I was no exception; he tried to make everyone. "Hey, Jimmy!" He put his arm around me and gave me a squeeze. "How's the boy? Hey, you look even fuckier than usual. Goddamn you!" On closer inspection he added: "Yeah, you do, but—hey, man, you look—are you all right?"

"Sure. Carmine, I bet you'd know. Where can I buy a gun?"

"A gun? Say, Jimmy, are you all right? I never saw you looking so—well, I don't know"—he ducked his head back away from me—"just kind of wild and woolly."

"Yeah, I'm fine. What about a gun?"

"A *gun*?"

"Oh, it's just—like for a joke, to surprise someone. Just a joke."

"Oh. I don't know, I guess a hock shop, pawnshop. Hey, Ginny Steeples is having a party, costume party, you remember where she lives over on West Tenth?" I nodded, Ginny Steeples had been in the same show I'd worked with Carmine in. "I know she'd like to have you come by. Come over, any time after ten thirty, will you?"

"If I can."

"Okay, try man, we'll put it together, have some fun. A lot of the old gang'll be there." He looked at me again and gave me another squeeze. "Hey, you look great, don't shave." He laughed and thumped me on the back. "Happy New Year! Come by Ginny's."

I said I'd try and went in search of pawnshops. In a half hour I'd found three; all were closed. I'd worked up a sweat and my head was covered with snow. The hell with a gun; I didn't need a gun. I headed west, stopped off at a grocery and delicatessen, and plodded my way in the snow back to Cork Street.

Up the first flight, then, as I climbed the second, I noticed light streaking out into the darkened hallway. I could hear music. I could also hear movement.

I don't believe it.

Quickly I put the groceries down, slipped off my shoes, and crept up to the third floor. The door was partly open. I peeked in.

Kate moved into sight, carrying something, her back to me, across the room near the bed. I opened the door wider and stood there quietly. She'd turned the clock radio on and didn't hear me. A second more and she must have sensed something, because she suddenly wheeled around. "Jim . . . !"

I'd forgotten how much her pure physical presence affected me. She looked gorgeous; she'd managed to get a slight tan, no more than a light beige glow. There was a split second when I almost splattered from joy and relief, when I wanted to grab her and hold on for three weeks.

What was all this craziness I'd been toying with, this drunken binge, this sitting in the dark waiting for burglars?

I began to walk toward her, to say, "Oh, God, it's so good to—"

She clutched the small zipper bag that held her cosmetics. It was not this that caused me to break off in mid-sentence, halt in mid-step, as much as the expression on her face. One of surprise and frustration and, unusual for Kate, embarrassment, all in all a look that made her features come unglued. The glow was smeared.

Her face was telling me too much. I glanced away; it was then I saw her "second" fur coat on the bed along with her ski clothes and her blue suitcase half opened, half packed with clothes she usually left at my apartment. A long and sickening silence filled the room.

Finally Kate spoke. "I called several times, no answer. I thought you'd already gone up to Claire's—"

"I take it you're going someplace, too." Kate glanced down at her hands. "Well, aren't you?" No reply. "Aren't you?"

A "Yes" from her, so quiet it panicked me.

"Yes," I echoed.

Then: "Jim, you look—you look *terrible*."

"Thank you."

"I don't mean, I mean—you look all—you don't have *shoes* on."

"Oh, yes . . ." I turned to go back down and get them and saw, on the long refectory table near the door, the portable television set Kate had given me as a Christmas present to replace the one taken in the second robbery. It had been moved from its place in the bookcase, the cord was wrapped around the handle. "Are we returning our Christmas gifts?"

"What?" she asked.

"I see you're taking the television."

"I'm taking the—what a stupid thing to say. I gave it to you as a *present*."

"What?" I asked. "It has a date for New Year's?" I turned to face the television set. "You stepping out again? I thought I told you—"

"Don't be ridiculous, I was not taking it!"

There was such an air of embarrassment about her that I included the television set in it.

On the same table, nearer the door, I saw a white envelope propped next to a vase. I picked it up. "Jim" was printed on it in Kate's hand. I tore it open.

"No, Jim, don't—!"

"Christ, it's addressed to me, isn't it?" I was shouting and it felt good.

"Jim, please, don't—"

"Please, *don't!* You—for God's sake, this is obviously, what do they call them, a Dear John? And you don't want me to *open* it? Who knows, I might even have a reply. You didn't want me to open it, you should have left instructions: Don't open until April Fuck Day!" I ripped it open and read. " 'Dear Jim!' Well, so far so good, it's not a laugh riot, but it's got a nice homey touch. It's sincere, to the point. Tell me, did you do this all by yourself?"

Suddenly she was laughing, really laughing, tilting her head back. "I always did get a kick out of you when you got mad. I actually think that's why I used to provoke fights, to get a peek at your nasty little sense of humor. Because in spite of your annoying— squareness, no, your insistence upon *staying* square—you do have a sense of humor."

"Whoopee!" I quickly tore the note into tiny pieces. "Right, you're right. I shouldn't read it. Why deprive you from telling me in person. Come on, let me hear it from your very own lips, in person."

Kate sighed. "Jim, let's not be mean."

"Let's not be *mean!* Who's walking out on who New Year's Eve?"

"I picked tonight because I knew you'd be going to your precious *Claire's* and, frankly, because I knew you'd be so preoccupied with the play the next couple of months, it probably wouldn't make all that much difference."

"Oh, *Kate!*"

"Oh, *Jim!* Come on, it's not as if it were news. We both knew it was coming. I thought this was the easiest way." Now a bit of the old nastiness slipped into her voice. "No problem accommodating Claire, no chance of disappointing her. I saw her telegram." When she caught the look on my face she added: "It was sitting *right there!*"

"Jesus, do we have to get into her again?"

"Why not? Everything you do is colored by her. Just think, two consenting adults, one thirty-eight—sorry, thirty-two"—she always did that, took delight in it—"the other thirty-three, keeping two separate apartments in this day and age. Because you knew Claire would shit little green apples if—"

"Charming."

"Sorry—*true!* Oh, I know what you said, because of the *book!* Did you think I'd stand around banging on pots and pans to keep you from working on it? Claire again. And that part in the movie, what about that?"

"The first movie I make I don't want to be standing on a cliff in Technicolor and Panavision with my three-piece set blowing in the wind."

A surprise grin from her; that's what I loved about her, the little surprises she could dish out. "It's a nifty three-piece set, take it from me."

I shook my head. "The way you talk sometimes, I wouldn't be surprised if *you* had one tucked away. You'd make a great agent, you're tough enough. You'd have me playing all fruits or nude scenes."

"Ah!" She thrust a finger at me; she had a way of thrusting a finger out, threatening impalement, that made me want to snap it off. "You were excited about that movie, it was about a guy about to commit suicide, not about a man standing on a cliff exposing himself. And *Boys in the Band*, you turned that down because Claire would have gone into cardiac arrest to see her nephew—So you stick to the safe things, that tired soap you did, your occasional summer tour in *Mary, Mary*, for God's sake."

"I'm not that much in demand, I don't get offered every choice role that comes along, you know!"

"Then you must be doing *something* wrong! You're attractive, you're at a good age, you're—"

"And you're a supreme pain in the ass, Kate!"

Kate sighed. "You may have something, let's leave it. I've dropped my bomb, and like any sensible bomber—I'll leave."

I went to make myself a drink. I could not tell her about the play falling through, could not put myself in the position of accepting sympathy from her. A final consoling pat on the shoulder as she walked out the door. I fixed her a drink, too, and took it to her as she finished packing. "No, thanks."

I shouted at her. "Oh, Jesus, take it, one for the bustup!"

She echoed my loudness. "All right, *all right!*"

She sipped, looked at me, and smiled. "I'm very happy about the play, Jim. I hope it does good things for you." I nodded; we drank. She cocked her head, then smiled again. "I never saw you look so—well, messed up, but—still . . ."

"What?"

"Scrummy, sort of like a rumpled bed. You *should* go around messed up a little, it looks good on you." The results were coming in, first Carmine, now Kate. She sipped her drink, then set her glass down with the resolve of a general. "I'm going to tell you something!"

"Oh, Jesus!"

"Yes, well, *Oh, Jesus, I am!* Somebody once said, 'That Jimmy Zoole, he's such an attractive guy. Say, are his front teeth capped?' The other person replied, 'Jimmy Zoole's *whole life is capped.*' "

"What is that supposed to mean?"

"It means you should look more like you do right now, you ought to shake yourself up a little, mix it up. Everything's so by the rule with you, so—now we lift our weights, now we have our singing lesson, now we learn our lines, now we—you try so *hard*. It hurts to watch you try so hard. Sometimes I'd just like to see you say the hell with it and—"

"What—smoke pot, I suppose?"

"No, I'm not talking about *that*! Although, yes, that's part of it, too."

"It doesn't work with me, you know that."

"Because you wouldn't *let it* work, you wouldn't let chloroform work!"

Oh, I was so weary of hearing from her! "Kate, tell me, do you have any *unuttered thoughts at all*? Do you, about me or Claire or acting or *anything*? Huh—do you?" She laughed. "My God," I said, "with all my faults, whatever made it work? Or were you faking all along?"

This took the steam out of her. "No," she sighed, "it worked, it sure did." She took a sip of her drink. "I was attracted to you because you were—good and clean and gracious and funny, and sad, too. And screwed up in your own tight little hidden way. And, funny, for anyone as filled to the brim with the Puritan ethic, you really do make the wildest Hugglebunnyburgers."

We smiled and made persimmon faces. "Ah," I groaned, "that is a brutal one, isn't it?"

"So disgusting, it's elevated to greatness," Kate said.

We spoke together. "Hugglebunnyburgers—feh!"

"Were they really that good?" I asked.

"Umm, that's what hooked me on you at first. We'd be out and you'd be so, oh, opening doors, overtipping, never giving a waitress or salesman back any of the lip they give out. Then we'd get home and into bed—it was like some dusty Italian workman had just been let loose from the marble quarry. I couldn't get over the difference, I used to get a terrific kick out of it."

She could pay a compliment where it counted. I decided to jump right in. "So, all right, move your things back to your place, but let's spend New Year's together. I'll call Claire and tell her I'm sick and—"

"See, that's what—you're a thirty-eight-year-old man, why wouldn't you just tell her you want to spend New Year's with your *girl!*"

"Why go out of my way to hurt her feelings?"

"She doesn't have any, the only feelings she's—"

"All right, I'll just tell her I can't make it!"

"No, I can't, Jim. Honestly, I can't."

I was amazed. "Then why go on so about it—about *her*, for God's sake?"

"It was agreed we'd spend New Year's apart so I—" Kate cleared her throat. "So—well, I made other plans."

There, that made a dent. "Oh, you made plans. Well, that's different." I could feel the anger rising from my locked knee-caps. "Plans, huh? What's his name—Johnnie Plans? Or *Joe* Plans?"

"I'm—we're just going to a dance tonight, then up to the Catskills tomorrow, skiing." She quickly added: "Just for the day."

"You and Mr. Plans? You mean you made a date with some guy, *then* you suggested we skip New Year's and—"

"No, it didn't happen like that, Jim. Please, give me that much—"

"Please, my ass!" I started pacing. "No wonder Claire was catching such hell. You had to dump it on someone. You're right, I'm square. Square? I'm *retarded*. You're probably in the middle of your next affair. Why the hell didn't you just tell me instead of letting me—Jesus, letting me crawl around on my knees!"

"Stop it, it wasn't like that. It's just someone I met through work and he asked me and I—"

"And you just—oh, shit—get out! What a dirty—"

"Jim, stop it!" she shouted.

I topped her by far. "GET OUT!"

As she hurried to assemble her things for a fast exit, I scrambled over to the bedside table, opened the bottom drawer, and took out her diaphragm, which she kept in a small plastic bag. I tossed it across the bed toward her. "Here, better take your equipment." I opened the top drawer, took out a tube of KY jelly, and flung that at her. "There, a strobe light and you're all set."

She knocked the diaphragm off onto the floor. "Keep it. I bought a new one."

"Charming. Just like you to say that."

She scooped up her things. As she walked toward the door, she muttered: "I'm sorry we had to have this—"

"If you'd have been honest, we wouldn't have. Aunt Claire, my ass! Cheap little horny—"

"Charming," she said, reaching for the door. "Goodbye."

"Goodbye and good luck!" I stood there and watched her leave, watched the door slam shut after her. I was dizzy with anger. I rushed to the door and snatched it open. "Skiing, eh?" I shouted at her disappearing figure down the stairs. "As they say in the theater—break a leg! Break *both* legs! That way you'll have an excuse for staying on your *back*!" Although I could no longer see her, I kept on shouting. "You've been a great pal on New Year's! I'll always remember you for your compassion and your goddamn boring-ass lectures!" I hurled my glass down the stairs after her. The crash at the bottom of the landing was pleasing to my ears. "Mazel tov! Lehaim! May all your orgasms turn to stone!"

I slammed the door, a wall-shaking slam. I walked, trembling, to the center of the room. I stood there shaking, shaking not only at her, but shaking now at the sight of the loser I beheld staring back at me—wild-eyed, yes—in the mirror over the mantel.

"You poor sad-assed excuse for an actor. Correction—for a human being."

Sanity advised me to avert my eyes *and* to stop talking to myself. I caught a glimpse of a framed color photograph of Kate and me taken on the beach at East Hampton. I quickly stepped to the mantel and smashed it on the floor. This small violence spurred me on. Rushing to the window, I thrust it open and jammed my head and shoulders out. There she was, scuttling across the street through the snow toward her car.

"Happy New Year!" I shouted. She stopped, turned and glanced up at me. "Wait! I've got something for you!"

"What . . . ?" she called up.

"*Wait!*" I shouted again. From the large bowl of fruit I kept on a table between the two windows, I snatched an apple and ducked out the window just as she called out "What?" again.

"Here!" I side-armed the apple at her. A miss, it struck the street a yard or so from her feet, but it elicited, to my ears, a pleasurable little cry of surprise as Kate turned and made for her car. I snatched up an orange and threw it hard. "Hey, here you go! Ah-hah!" It glanced off the side of the suitcase she carried. Now a sharper cry escaped her. She steadied herself, turned, and squinted up through the snow at me.

"Jimmy . . . ?" she called out. Translation: Are you all right?

"Go with Christ!" I yelled. I grabbed a banana and held it out the window. "You know what you can do with this!" I hurled it end-over-end. Kate turned away to avoid flying objects, slipped or tripped, and in regaining her balance dropped the fur coat she'd been carrying slung over her shoulder. It lay crumpled in the snow.

"Ahh!" she cried, setting down the suitcase and picking up her coat. "Bastard!" she yelled, without looking up at me.

This earned a chortle. "Dropped her goddamn fur coat!" Next I hurled a fistful of three lemons at random. One of them connected with its target, striking her in the lower back. "Jim! Stop it—what's the—*stop it!*"

She quickly shook off her coat, picked up her suitcase, and hurried toward the car. "That's right, hustle it up!" I called. I hit the side of the car with a tangerine, just as she opened the door. She cried out in annoyance, quickly tossing her things in the car and scrambling in herself.

"Farewell, my little hummingbird! Don't take any wooden Hugglebunnyburgers!"

No fun, now that she was inside the car. I withdrew from the window, closed it, and walked back to the center of the room. I was still shaking, but shaking now from a certain exuberance achieved by throwing assorted fruit down at my ex-love. I caught sight of my flushed face in the mirror. "Jesus, Aunt Jemima, move over!" Then: "Am I flipping?" I stepped up close to the mirror, as if I might receive an answer. I kept staring at myself, until I noticed my trembling again. The sight was not reassuring. I turned away.

I needed distraction from myself. I knew if I should get lured back to the mirror I was in trouble. I went to the torn bits of Kate's letter and picked them up, putting the pieces in a clean ashtray on the table near the door. Now that I was unemployed this might be a good project for some long winter evening, a sort of Dear John Jigsaw Puzzle.

On the far side of the television set on this same table, there was a large china bowl; in it I had thrown all my Christmas cards. As I went to pick the television up to move it back to the bookcase, something black caught my eye, something lying in with the mass of cards. At first I thought it was a piece of pipe sticking up.

I stepped closer to the bowl and looked down at the coal black object lying partly obscured by several Christmas cards. I picked it up—by what turned out to be the barrel. A gun, it was a pistol of some sort.

No, wait a minute—I'd been looking for a gun and now I find one *in the bowl with my Christmas cards*? I had to shake my head to clear it. What *was* this?

I had never owned a gun, nor to my knowledge had Kate. I knew little about them. I changed my hold on it, now grasping it by the handle. It was no toy gun, it was heavy and lethal-looking.

The phone rang; I must have jumped a foot or so. It was Claire, speaking in a brittle annoyed voice that wanted, once it got over giving me hell for being unreachable, to lapse into a neglected whine. The last thing I needed was a long one-way conversation with her, not now, standing there with a gun in my hand at the end of a most peculiar day. I blurted it out: "Claire, I was just about to call you. I'm sorry but I can't come. I—"

"Can't come? But you promised, I'm leaving tomorrow. We won't get a chance to see each other."

"Claire, listen to me, just for a minute. I got—"

"It's Kate, isn't it? Of course, it is. Well, you can be with her *all* the time, but—"

I tried to speak but she went on. She had a way by *not listening* of blasting her way through rock and achieving her end. Suddenly the light years of her voice ganged up on me. I was struck allergic to the sound of her, just as someone suddenly bloats up from a shot of penicillin. "Claire, listen to me now. *Listen!*"

"I will, dear. But I know it's Kate. Just as well as I know, having promised, you won't—"

"Jesus, *Jesus!*" I slammed the phone down. "Deaf goddamn pussy! Deaf! Jesus, her *deafness!*" I stood my ground, gun still in hand. I knew the phone would ring back and it did. I picked it up. "I won't apologize for that, I hope I made my point, please listen to me now! I *got fired from the play*! On top of that Kate and—"

"Fired from the play, but rehearsals haven't even started. That's ridiculous!"

"Not quite my reaction and I'm not finished yet by a long—"

"I don't know what you're *talking* about."

"—Because you won't listen! If you'd—"

"Jimmy, you just come right up here and tell me all—"

"Oh, dear Jesus God in Christ!" I slammed the phone down. I couldn't go it with her, simply could not make it through the nattering.

The phone rang again. I walked away from it, once again looking at the gun in my hand. Ring, ring, ring, ring! The ringing suddenly drove me wild—a swarm of buzzing ringing Claires trying to get at me.

I spun around, aimed, and fired at the phone. A shot blasted from the gun, jerking my arm back and stunning me. The bullet struck the desk, ricocheted over to the wall—a drift of white powder sprang from the red of the brick—and went on about its way, I couldn't track it.

Then I heard, from somewhere terribly near, a man's voice: "Okay, okay, take it easy. Take it easy!"

I wheeled around—I'd been standing near the sofa and the voice had come from behind me—as it said, "Okay, guy, take it easy!" And there, two legs scuttled out from under the bed and next there came a waist in view and a chest and the voice kept on: "Okay, okay, don't do nothin'! I give up!"

The phone kept ringing. My *head* was ringing. I could only think: Yes, I've finally been struck crazy. Hallucinating. The day should have been dead, dead as a duck, ended. No, wait a minute, *I was waiting to surprise the burglar!*

But now—*who was this coming out from under the bed?*

I stood there holding the gun while a neck and then his face appeared. Talking all the while in a hoarse tough voice, lessened in its toughness by the jagged edge of fright. "Take it easy, take it easy! Okay, it's a draw, I didn't take nothin'—okay?"

He was asking me. Young, under thirty, rugged. But scared, he was scared. And I had the gun.

The phone stopped ringing. The pieces jogged together in my

head. The television set by the door, the gun—My God and Jesus H. Unbelievable Christ, I was being robbed again. But—

Now he'd slid himself out from under the bed. He lay on the floor, hands with their backs to his chest, palms up in place for doing push-ups into the air—the classic holdup position only horizontal—ready to ward off any action I might take against him.

"Take it easy, it's a draw, no harm done, I didn't take nothin'. Right after I—down through there"—he bobbed his head in the direction of the skylight—"she come, surprised me, I left the gun by the TV. Ducked under the bed. Then you come. I didn't take nothin'. My mother's grave." He crossed himself.

When I didn't say anything because I *couldn't*, he went on: "Just let me outta here, okay?" He started to get up, swiveled over, got on one knee. "Okay?"

I aimed the gun at him. *"Let you outta here?"*

I thought the gun would stop him; it did for a second, but then he was up on his feet, circling me slowly in a crouch, keeping his distance, moving over by the bookcases, his eye on the door. "Okay, you had it rough, I heard all that shit, *I* had it rough. It's a draw, just let me outta here." He kept moving.

"Stop! *Stop!*" I kept the gun on him.

"Forget the gun," he said. "There was only one bullet!" With that he made for the door.

Again I shouted for him to stop. When he paid no attention I aimed down at his legs and pulled the trigger. There was a loud click.

He glanced back, saw what I'd done, said, "Crazy bastard!" and reached out for the door handle. I threw the gun at him with all my might. It crashed against the door to the right of his head, only inches away, and fell to the floor. He lurched sideways; I'd made him miss the knob.

"You—you fucking *robber*!" And I was after him.

I know exactly what temporary insanity means, feels like, is.

What it is, is not knowing and, above all, not caring. It is simply—
doing.

I grabbed him by his three-quarter-length jacket and tore him down, wrenched him to the floor, then hit him. To kill him, pulverize him, was my intent, rip him to pieces.

In terror, he flipped me off him and tried to scramble away. I grabbed him with both hands, wrenched him over and threw my full weight on top of him. He was shorter, more wiry, harder, and younger than me but he was no match. His panic weakened him, just as my fury strengthened me.

He screamed even louder now, screamed for help, screamed for mercy, and now that we were face-to-face close, his screaming hurt my ears. I wanted to quiet him, so I went for his throat and I connected. I dug my fingers into his neck—oh, the feeling, like kneading tough dough, pure tactile joy—and I started closing on the tenseness, on the straining veins and muscles of this very frightened being underneath me.

Terror glazed his eyes as he began to choke. His eyes bulged out dangerously, looked as if they might actually pop. I believe I would have cut off his breath entirely if I hadn't been stopped by the startling greenness of his eyes, the same sea-green as Kate's.

How can one be struck by such a detail at a time like that? I don't know, I can only report that I was. They were Kate's eyes, large, grainy blue-green and cat-shaped even though they bulged. I must have eased off my pressure, because now I could understand his choked words.

"Quit-it, quit, ogg-god, quit!"

I shouted down into his face. "Quit it, *quit it*—why should I quit it!"

He could barely speak. I let up a little more. He coughed, gagged some, coughed again. "Why should I quit it—you no-good fucking little bastard!"

"Because—" he gasped. He sucked in breath, then exhaled: "For the main reason—it hurts."

Even then, with me in my condition and especially with him in his, the sentence grabbed my attention. The wording, the phrase struck me wildly funny. I repeated it: *"For the main reason—it hurts?"*

My laughter confused him. Strangely enough, this confusion made him look almost bearably human. I didn't like it. I applied pressure again. He saw I meant business and this brief respite had allowed for some strength to seep back into him. He put every ounce of it to use and managed to twist me off, throwing me sideways and thumping into the wall. Before he could gain solid footing I reached out and caught him by the leg with one hand. He scrambled away a few yards, dragging me with him until I finally caught hold of him with my other hand and jerked him back down again.

Now neither of us yelled or screamed. No time for words. We were down to the serious business of finishing this competition off. No way would he escape me. If he were to somehow get out of the apartment, I knew I would chase him on foot to California if need be.

I tried once more to lurch forward, to get on top of him, as we wrestled across the floor. By now he was infected with terror. We knocked over an end table next to an easy chair, sending it and a lamp crashing to the floor.

I ducked to avoid the falling lamp and this diversion allowed him to get to his feet again. He made for the bathroom door directly ahead of him. I lunged after him, got him around the waist in a flying tackle, and the two of us crashed up against the built-in bookcase abutting the wall next to the bathroom door.

Because he was in front of me, he bore the brunt of the crash. It dazed him and he fell to his knees. I grabbed him by the shoulders, spinning him around and slamming him down. He was now in a sitting position by the corner of the bookcase. He shook his head, put his hand up to his forehead, shook it again, and blinked his eyes. I dropped to my knees in front of him. My barbell weight was directly behind his head, standing on end, resting up against the corner of the bookcase and the wall.

He opened his eyes wide, focused, looked directly at me, then spit in my face. The final indignity. I grabbed him by the shoulders, swung him forward toward me to gain momentum, then slammed his head back against the long iron pole of the barbell.

A terrible dull bonking-thud sounded. His head dropped to the side, hit his shoulder, seemed to bounce off it, then hung down to the side of his chest.

Jesus, I got him, I had him, I'd won! There was fright in it and wonder and excitement. Excitement! To me, a non-fighter, it was thrilling. Not only to fight but to win!

There was too much excitement to stay still. I stood up, just to have movement, and stepped back away from him, this human being I'd turned into a body.

Soon the excitement, the thrill of beating him, was on the wane, replaced by fear that I might have killed him. Of course I wanted to *murder* him—but not really kill him, dead, for all times!

This person, I didn't even know him . . .

I caught myself wondering right at that moment if he had a family, a wife and children. And the phrase "Head of Household" hit me. Have I killed Head of Household?

The hang of his head looked precariously uncomfortable, as if, if he *weren't* dead, his neck might break from the weight of it. I knelt down, quickly took him by the shoulders, and eased him out flat on the floor.

The phone rang. From reflex I got up, turned, and stepped toward it. No—oh, no, none of that. It only rang six or seven times.

When it stopped I stood there, still breathing heavily, feeling a need to connect with reality. I glanced around the room, at the television set, at the large ashtray that held the bits and pieces of Kate's letter, at Bobby Seale's water and food bowls; my eyes touched on a sort of cloudy reality, too: the gouge in the wood where the gun had struck the door, the gun itself, on the floor over by the corner of the bookcase, the broken end table, and the smashed lamp.

Anger returned, anger that not only was I being robbed *again*, but he had been under the bed eavesdropping into my personal life. Jesus!

I looked back at him. He fit in perfectly with the mess, he was garbage. I walked back and stood staring down at his limp form. I do not boast of my actions now. I suddenly kicked him in the side. Not a gentle kick either. "Bastard!" I swung my foot back again but stopped. There was still the possibility that he might be dead. No use kicking a dead man.

I knelt by him and lifted his head to see if it might possibly be cracked open. Tilting him, I inspected for damage. His hair was dark brown, thick, long but not hippyish, and, by this time, completely disheveled. I could feel the large lump even before I parted the hairs with my fingers. It was a nasty bruised ridge, already discoloring and only faintly smudged with blood from the pores, but it was not split open, not openly bleeding.

After letting his head rest back on the rug, I bent down close to him. His mouth was slightly open. I could barely tell if he was breathing. I opened his jacket and placed a hand on his chest. There was movement, slight but it was there, faintly in and out. No dead bodies, praise be for that.

I stood up. Manic, once again, and thinking now of Pete, if he were alive. How great to call up and say: "Hey, Pete, get your ass over here, see what I got!"

Yes, see what I got. But what to do with the miserable robbing bastard? God's truth, I never once thought of calling the police. I could simply drag him downstairs and throw him out into the street with the garbage. No, careful. I'd be an easy target for reprisals once he came to.

I thought of the basement, that was an idea. I had a key to the heavy latch-type lock and the door itself was metal, inside at the far end of the ground-floor hallway, now completely unoccupied. Only one small barrel slit of a window looked up at the back alley shared with a dilapidated, defunct warehouse. No one would hear him. I caught a picture of him down there, shouting, eventually pleading, clawing at the door like some trapped animal.

I laughed. Kate often referred to me as her "square lover." I was not feeling square now. My imagination was most certainly not pointed at square. I'd played by the rules long enough and been called out more often than not. I'd play by my own rules now. I might even make up a few new ones.

Still, the question of what to do with him. The basement intrigued me. It was a scary place, damp and dark. I'd never been comfortable when I'd made brief trips down there to find out why there was no hot water or to change a blown fuse.

Then, in opposition to my imagination, my square-headed pedestrian logical boring mind interrupted: What if I did make him prisoner down there? Would he, out of desperation, play havoc with the furnace, the hot-water heater, or the fuse box? Surely he would. Though bereft of outside help or his burglar's tools, he would not be stripped of the same ingenuity that enabled him to rob apartments.

Annoyed with myself for letting logic interfere, I was even more annoyed with *him,* lying there so patiently on the floor. I thought of kicking him again. But why kick him if he couldn't feel it?

What if he was the same burglar who'd robbed me twice before? What if he, lying right down at my feet, had taken my pages? In a way it made sense—once you'd latched onto a good deal, why not milk it dry? Top floor, no doorman, no one else in the entire building to disturb a burglar in the middle of his work. The idea made the blood rush to my face.

I nixed the basement. I would be forfeiting all active participation if I should lock him up down there. Oh, Jesus Christ and all the disciples, if he should be the one! Even if he shouldn't, he had every right to stand in as proxy. I wanted my full licks. I definitely should be in attendance at any punishment I might devise for him.

I looked outside the window. The snow fell so thickly now; the air between was barely visible, it was all snow. A great rush of coziness enveloped me at being inside my apartment with—what?— well, my consolation prize, my prisoner, stretched out so completely at my disposal. Again I thought of Pete. There was a strong impulse to call someone, let someone know. It was an unusual event and unusual events should be shared. "Hello, *New York Times*. Listen—" Not practical, though.

Still, it was cause for celebration. I quickly fixed myself a drink of scotch. I walked to the mirror and toasted myself. "That'll teach 'em to fuck around with you!" All right, what to do with him? No point drinking and stalling around until he comes to. I glanced around the room and then it hit me. Yes, I knew what to do, how I would celebrate the New Year. We would celebrate it together, albeit in different circumstances.

I giggled. I remember hearing my giggle, realizing *he* couldn't hear it, that no one could. And I thought: This is not like me! Not at all.

This did not, however, cause me undue worry.

When I'd first moved into the loft there'd been only the most makeshift kitchen stuck off in a corner: small stove and refrigerator, small built-in counter and porcelain-topped kitchen table. There was no running water, the dishes had to be washed in the bathroom sink.

When Claire came to see the place, right after I'd moved in, she offered to donate a proper kitchen unit. Because of the unorthodoxy of construction and plumbing in the building, I was able to have a large free-standing butcher-block, combined stainless-steel sink unit installed to connect with the downstairs plumbing. It stood some six feet out from the nearest wall, into which I'd had fitted a fine gas stove and wall oven, a proper refrigerator, and kitchen cabinets I'd built myself. It was now a splendid kitchen section, taking up about one sixth of the total loft.

The butcher-block unit struck me as the perfect place to strap him down to. I could place him belly down on it. Sturdy as it was, no amount of wriggling or twisting would matter.

I wondered how long a knocked-out person remains unconscious. Minutes or would it be an hour? No use taking chances.

It became a game. I tore around the apartment collecting odd pieces of rope that had been used to secure the two skylights before I'd had chains attached. Kate had dipped into macrame and she'd done two long "pulls" when she first started. These were usable, too, as were a few old ties and an old belt of mine.

First I removed his shoes and bound his ankles tightly, in case he should come to while I was still securing him to the butcher block. With effort I managed to turn him over and get his jacket off, ridding him of some bulk. Before I attempted to move him, I studied him closely for any signs of consciousness. He was still soundly elsewhere. I picked him up—he was heavier than he looked to be or perhaps it was the deadness of his weight—and carried him to the kitchen.

It was eerie, holding someone in my arms that I didn't know.

Holding someone in my arms—a phrase of closeness, affection even. None of this, of course, but there was a certain intimacy that was, well, eerie.

I was glad to be rid of him when I rolled him out of my arms onto his stomach, so that his thighs and legs were on one section of the butcher block, his middle straddled the sink, and his chest, arms, and head rested on the second section of the butcher block. Before trussing him up, I emptied his pants pockets: twenty-seven dollars, some change, three keys, a handkerchief, and a small pocket comb. He would be the type to carry a pocket comb. I could imagine him combing his hair in public, walking down the street and glancing in store windows to see his reflection.

Then I quickly tied his hands behind him, binding his wrists securely. Even if he came to before I had him strapped down, he would be helpless.

It was exciting, this operation, so much so that I went to the stereo to put on some records. Something big was called for; I chose *Aïda*, the Leontyne Price recording. Music to Tie People Up By.

A sip of my drink, then back to the task. I strapped him securely to the butcher block by taking one of the kitchen drawers out and passing the rope through the opening it afforded and around back of his knees. I passed another rope around the small of his back and brought it up and around the indentation under the sink itself. Now he was completely trussed up and strapped down. No amount of maneuvering could possibly help.

I stepped back, filled with pride at the excellent job of packaging. I was also filled with anticipation. I freshened my drink and pulled up a chair to sit directly in front of my home-made version of Gulliver.

His head rested cheek down on the butcher block. In order to have a better look at him I got a cushion from the sofa and put it under his chin, turning his head to the front, facing me. His eyes were closed, but I'd already taken them in, the large catlike green-blueness that reminded me so of Kate.

I brushed his hair back with my hand. His forehead was wide, the nose good-sized, not big, but the bridge was somewhat thicker than it should have been for the rest of it. It looked as if it might have been broken and mended thick. The cheekbones were high, prominent, the cheeks hollowing down where the mouth began. His lips were full and well formed; the bottom one seemed to have a small pout pocket right in the center. His chin squared off at the bottom, somewhat narrow, but not weak. All in all, a good-looking face, the main features being the eyes and his cheekbones.

Still, there was something scroungy about him. His complexion was medium, not dark, more fair, not peachy by any means, with a few faint freckles, and one small angled scar under his left eye, no more than half an inch long. Perhaps it was the scar that gave him a tomcattish look. Also, right now, one of his eyeteeth stuck out over his lower lip. He did remind me of a tomcat, a stringy one—he was lean for his size, which I guessed to be about five ten—a cat who'd been through his share of scrapes.

Despite the cold, he wore only a brown and black small-checked shirt underneath the three-quarter-length outer jacket. His pants were dark brown and expensive, I could tell, slightly belled at the bottom. His brown shoes, I'd noticed when I'd taken them off, were also expensive. This was one cat who cared about his appearance.

I sipped my drink, waiting for him to show signs of consciousness and wondering whether people who were knocked out dreamed. And whether he would remember clearly what happened or even where he was when he first awakened. Most of all, I wondered what his reactions would be.

The phone rang, I decided to answer, surely it would be Claire. It was. Her voice was chilly as she asked if I was all right. I told her I was simply not feeling well, *inside*, and, of course, apologized for hanging up on her.

"It certainly wasn't like you, Jimmy. I hope you're feeling better now. You shouldn't be alone if you're feeling blue, that's the only reason I wanted you to come up. Then, of course, you have Kate."

I told her Kate and I had broken up. This news brought a bit of warmth back into her voice. She doubted it was for good, but I assured her it most likely was. Then she thought she'd just let me in on "all the things I've held back from saying about that girl" but I cut her off and told her about the play falling through. There was sympathy but I could tell she was not destroyed by it. It gave her a chance to say once more, "When things like that happen, that's when it's good to have family. We have each other, it's good to know that."

As she talked on I glanced over at the body lying all tied up over the sink. There was a certain perverse titillation in talking to Claire on the phone with him lying there like that. *Oh, Claire, if you only knew*. She asked me again to come up to her party but I told her I was going to bed early. It must have been the news about Kate that permitted Claire to let me off the hook as easily as she did. We said our good nights and I hung up.

It was only then that I remembered my shoes were still down on the second floor along with the groceries. I brought them up, unpacked the food, and sat down once more in front of—I wondered what his name was.

I sat there for a long time.

When he first started to stir, a blink or two of the eye, a twitch, then a slight pucker and a lick of his lips, I glanced at the clock. It was nine fifteen.

Sitting on a kitchen chair, backward, my chin resting on the back of it, I was perhaps three feet directly in front of him.

He licked his lips again; his eyetooth, the one that had been protruding, disappeared. "Mnn..."—a small sleep sound. He coughed, then turned his head slowly to the side, so that his cheek rested on the pillow. This small movement must have been a strain of sorts, he must have noticed the pull from his hands being tied behind him. He opened his eyes, looked at his shoulder, saw his arm stretching behind him, then suddenly, in his peripheral vision, caught sight of something in front of him.

He turned his head front. "Ahh!" The nearness of a strange person startled him. As much as he could, he ducked his head back. "Oh..." He blinked his eyes again, then focused on me. "Uh?" Then the circumstances came back to him. "Oh, Jesus!" He tried to get up but, of course, he could barely move. He made several wrenching movements, but it was no use. "What?" He turned his head, looked to the right, facing the kitchen cabinets and the spice racks, then swiveled his head back around the other way toward the living-room area.

He looked back at me. I returned his gaze, as impassively as I could. I made a good show of it, although inside I was far from impassive.

Once again he glanced at his right shoulder, made an effort to see up and over it, to discover just how his hands were tied. When he looked back at me, he finally spoke. "Jesus, what is this—the end of the world!" I didn't reply. "Huh?" he asked.

I kept staring at him. He turned his head to the left, once again looking toward the living room. This caused him to groan. "Oww, Christ, my head!" Back to me. "Jesus, you doused my fuckin' lights."

I noticed another small scar, this one over his right eyebrow, noticed it when he wrinkled his forehead and asked a direct question in a straightforward manner that indicated he expected a logical answer. "Hey, what'd you tie me down for—huh?"

The answer was so obvious that I smiled. "That's funny?" he asked. "Hey, answer me, what'd you go and tie me down for?" Suddenly he gasped. "Jesus, you didn't call the cops, did you? *Did you?* Listen, I got—I got twenty-seven bucks in my pocket—" Then, as if it had just occurred to him: "Hey, you took my coat off. Okay, you can have the money and I got two ounces of pot, cleaned, really good stuff, in my jacket pocket. You can have that, too—just let me outta here." When I didn't answer, he said, "Come on, guy, I didn't do nothin' to you."

His speech was incredible, a take-off on the fierce New Yorkese seldom heard for real. His d's turned to t's. "I didn't do nothin'" sounded "I dit-unt do nut-in'."

"Jesus," he said, "if you called the cops! What a shitty thing to do on New Year's! Hey, guy, did youse call 'em?" (I smiled: *no one* says "youse" any more.) "Come on, give a guy a break! It's New Year's Eve." I sat there, still with my chin resting on the back of the chair. I could tell my silence was getting to him. "Hey, answer me!" he shouted. The shouting caused him to groan again. "Ooow, my head! Hey, you there—ah, yeah, *Jimmy*—that's it—hey, Jimmy?" (He gave it two syllables—Jim-may.)

His use of my first name struck me oddly. First, his even knowing it threw me off for a split second until I realized he'd been under the bed all the while Kate and I were having at it. More than that, he spoke my name with complete familiarity, as if he were a friend.

He cocked his head. "What? You're not talkin' to me, huh? Is that it? Big deal. You womp the shit outta me, knock me the fuck out, tie me up—and *you're not talkin' to me*? BFD—Big Fuckin' Deal." A beat, then: *"I shouldn't be talkin' to you!"* He waited for a reply; he got none. "Is that the big scoop? You're not talkin' to me?"

The phone, across the room from the kitchen area, rang. As I walked to it, he, this character, said, "If that's my old lady, don't tell her I'm here. She don't like you!"

The cat had a sense of humor.

Kate's voice on the phone, tentative: "Jim . . . ?"

"Oh, hi, ah—Kate, isn't it? I remember you, big eyes, big mouth."

"Don't be smart," she said. "Are you all right?"

"Never better, why?"

"*Why?* Throwing things out the window, all that yelling, I got worried, that's why."

A shout from the prisoner. "Hey! He-ee-ey!"

I cupped my hand over the mouthpiece. "Shut up!" Then, to Kate. "So, what's up with you?"

Now a barrage of shouting from the kitchen. "Help! HELP! This crazy nut has me tied up! H-E-L-P! Goddamnit—help!"

From Kate: "What's all the—what's *that*?"

"That—oh, *that*? Just some ratty little crum-bum burglar I caught."

"Stop kidding," she said, impatiently.

"Help! HELP!" he shouted again.

"I'm not kidding."

"You've got to be—A *burglar*!" she snorted.

"I'm not kidding," I repeated.

He bellowed: *"He's not kidding, goddamnit!"*

A pause, then Kate asked: "Jim, what's going on there?"

"I told you, I caught a burglar."

"Oh, Jim—"

"Well, you asked me and I'm telling you."

A sigh. "All right, you caught a burglar and—*what* are you doing with him?"

"I've got him tied up."

"He's got me tied up!" he shouted. Then: "Oh, shit!"

"Did you hear that?" I asked her.

"I hear yelling." She cleared her throat and when she spoke again her voice was extremely patronizing. "All right, you caught a burglar and you tied him up and *now* what?"

I spoke more for his benefit than for hers although I realized I was having it off both ways. Along about this time, I was feeling extremely heady, I admit. "What am I going to do with him? Hmn, I'm not sure yet. Torture him maybe, or—maybe just a good clean kill and dispose of the body. Or, perhaps, a little experimenting. After all, I did study to be a doctor." (This was a lie but I thought it would be interesting for his ears.) "I still have my scalpels and everything. Might be good to keep in practice."

"Jimmy," Kate sighed, "stop the kidding, now I know you're kidding. What's the—"

"I'm not kidding! After all, who would know he was here? Burglars don't leave word when they're going to knock off a place. The way I figure, I'm home free."

"Then you're drunk," she said.

"I'm not drunk and I'm not kidding," I assured her.

He returned to the act, shouting again. "He's not kidding, goddamnit! Help me! *Get some goddamn help!*"

"So, who do you think that is—*Claire?*" I asked.

"Don't be ridiculous," she snapped. Still confused, she added: "I don't know, it could be the television for all I know."

I held the receiver out toward the kitchen. "She thinks you're the television," I said.

"Fuckin' nut!" he shouted.

I spoke to Kate. "Did you hear that?"

"Yes," she said, now more confused.

"Well, they don't say 'fuckin'' on TV. In the movies, on the stage, in the street, in the home, but not quite yet on TV. I expect it's coming soon, though."

"All right," she sighed. "You've got *someone* there, you're pulling some sort of an act. Who is it? What's his name?"

"I don't know, wait a minute." I turned to him. "We have a request. What's your name?"

"None of your fuckin' business," he said, in all nastiness.

"Hold on." I put the phone down, walked to the kitchen, picked up a large glass, filled it with water and sloshed it over his head. He cried out, swearing in anger. I cut him off with a warning. "The next batch will be *hot*! So careful the way you talk to me. Remember, you're not in the best of positions, you're not sitting in the catbird seat."

"Huh?" he muttered, his face dripping water.

"Forget it," I returned to the phone.

"There's really somebody there," Kate said.

"That didn't take too long to sink in, did it?"

"All right," she snapped, "but what are you *doing*?"

"Talking to *you*, right now. As to what I'm *going* to do— undecided. Who knows? I may cut him up in little pieces, wrap him in newspaper and deposit him in various garbage cans around the city. Remember when that sort of thing was popular?"

"Oh, well, you're just—"

"And so are you," I told her. Wanting to leave her in a complete muddle, I abruptly wound up the conversation: "Call me when you get back from skiing and I'll let you know the final results. Oh, and watch that last jump, it's a bitch!"

One last bellow of "HELP!" from the prisoner as I hung up.

The phone rang back immediately. I picked it up.

"Jim, are you all right? I don't get what—"

I cut her off. "Kate, I'm really very busy right now." I used her line. "We'll talk." And hung up again.

I turned around and smiled at him. "Enough of that, eh? Now back to *you*."

Oh, the joy in confusing Kate! She, who knew it all. I was a huge one-up on her now. This put me in a wildly happy mood. Celebration was called for; I took a bottle of champagne out of the refrigerator and began working the cork out. His eyes were on me, watching every move. When the cork popped, he uttered a deadpan "Whoopee."

I poured a glass and while I sipped it, I caught sight of his outer jacket there on the floor where I'd left it. I'd neglected to look in those pockets. When he saw what I was doing he muttered, "Help yourself."

The pockets yielded another comb, a good-sized cellophane packet containing pot and cigarette papers, a regular pack of cigarettes, a great tangle of keys on a ring, and a postcard from Rome of Michelangelo's *David*. The message read: "Dear Vito, I hope this card gets your postman hot! Hah-hah!" Signed "Cha-cha." It was addressed to Vito Antenucci, c/o Frazier, to a number way east on Seventh Street.

"So—Vito Antenucci."

"Yeah," he said, flatly. "Big fuckin' detective." (Pronounced de-teck-a-tive.)

There was one other item, a small white card, the size of a file card with such minuscule handwriting in ink that I had to get my reading glasses to make it out. On the top of the side I happened to look at was written Jokes. Underneath:

Why gypsies noisy lovers?—crystal balls
75 year old Navajo virgin
3 roosters—Little Red Hen
Drunk lady—bar—canary
Drunk fag—graveyard—kicked all your dirt off, silly
English TV quiz—niggercock
Black & White & Gray? Sister Mary Elephant
Bee-keeper, 250,000 bees—cigar box—fuck 'em
What has 3 cherries & dances? 20,000 chorus girls
2 goldfish in bowl—if no God, who changes water?
Why rub shit on altar Italian wedding? Keep flies off bride
How many Poles pull off kidnaping? 47. 2 to snatch kid, 45 to write
    note
Why so few Puerto Rican suicides? Not easy jump out basement window
Irish, Protestant, Jew—go to heaven
Jewish Santa Claus down chimney—Ho-ho-ho, anybody wanna buy any
    toys?

Maybe I had Bob Hope tied up to my kitchen sink. "You must be a regular card," I told him.

"Yeah, hah-hah!" he said. "Hey, who was that on the phone, the ballbreaker?"

Although I spoke facetiously, I didn't expect him to catch it. "Don't talk about my girl like that!" I quickly walked to him and flicked the remains of my drink in his face.

He sputtered, coughed, shook his head, then, after a string of cursing, said, "My luck to get mixed up with a *nut*! Jesus, eighty-six the booze for the Big Actor." A derisive sneer crept into his voice. "Your *girl*, your girl gave youse the old heave-ho." He spoke more to himself next. "Jesus, my luck. Vito-baby, you done it again. Wouldn't I pick a nut! My ever-grabbin' luck!"

There was a whine to his voice, the whine of one who plays at his underdogmanship.

"Your *luck*! Who asked you to drop in, Vito-baby? Okay, so pay the consequences, you crum."

This got a quick reaction. "Don't call me crum!"

The sentence carried an implied threat. "Or what?" I asked.

"Or *what*?"

"Yes—or what'll you do? You couldn't tie your *shoelace* now."

"Look who's talkin', the big outta-work actor. I heard you, you lost your fuckin' job!"

Oh, he was meddling in dangerous territory. "Crummy crum, as if you could do anything about anything. You couldn't even pick your nose, which is something you're undoubtedly extremely good at."

He spoke in real distaste. "Uhh! That's disgusting."

"Ahh! His Italian Lordship is offended." I laughed.

His cat eyes focused on me, as if studying me for the first time. "You know something—you got a mean streak!" The seriousness with which he delivered this conclusion struck me funny. My laughter annoyed him.

"You oughta see a shrink. You fucked-up excuse for a flop actor!"

The gall of his words, in his position, infuriated me. "You punk. You little no-good petty goddamn punk robber. You come sneaking in with a gun and—I'll bet you're the same dirty little bastard that robbed me twice before, aren't you?" I grabbed his tied-up wrists. *"Aren't you?"*

"No, honest-to-God, no!" I twisted his arms. "Jesus, no, let up!"

I applied more pressure. *"Aren't you?"*

"No, cut it out! Jesus, I was never here before. My mother's word of honor!"

I let go of his arms and faced him. There was something humiliating in his having overheard personal information regarding my life and times. I wanted to humiliate him in return, break him down completely. "Your *mother*, your mother's probably a cheap hooker!"

He made a bold attempt to spit in my face. Because his position denied him leverage, it hit my chest. I slapped him hard on the side of the head. The yowl, pure animal hurt, thrilled me. The shock I experienced from acknowledging the thrill doubled it, made it shimmer. I could feel the hairs rise on my arms. (I don't brag about my behavior, only report it.)

"Crum!" I screamed down at him.

"I'll kill you!" he shouted back.

"Kill me? Try a *cockroach*!" I grabbed his hands and twisted his arms again. "Jesus, I'll bet you're a junkie, too."

"Leave me *alone*." The whine again. "I ain't no junkie."

"You ain't no English teacher either!" I flung his arms down. "Rotten little punk burglar. And you call *me* fucked up, I ought to see a shrink! You ought to be put away, you little—what is it you like to be called? Crum? You crummy little bastard with a hooker for a mother! Where's your mother tonight? Out hooking for New Year's?"

"My mother's dead." He said it quietly, solemnly; I could tell by his tone he expected to stop me.

Not a chance. "Screwed herself to death, did she?"

"Oh, boy," he said. "I may be dumb and a few other things, but you—you know what you are? You're perverse!"

I laughed. "*Perverse*, am I? Ah-hah, we've been sneaking into the dictionary, haven't we?"

"You prick! I'm not gonna talk to you no more."

"Oh, Jesus, you've got to be kidding." I walked away from him, spun around, hand to my chest. "Break my heart, would you? And on New Year's? He's not going to talk to me." I held an imaginary gun to my forehead. "There's no reason to go on living. So long, Mom. Farewell, world!" I pulled the trigger—click!

He was watching. There was a grin behind his eyes; his face

masked it, but it was there behind his eyes. "You're some card. Yeah, the ace of spades, the death"—pronounced dett—"card."

I reminded him of his vow. "Thought you weren't going to talk."

"I'm not. For the main reason—you're nuts. No use talkin' to a crazy person."

"Remember, if you decide to break your pledge—you have to say 'May I?' "

"Nut," he muttered.

He was silent, so was I. I realized we were acting childishly, perhaps only I was, but it made no difference. There was an elation in having him captive that encouraged irrational behavior. However, this foray in total indulgence was tiring and the drinks I'd downed had weakened me. Hungry, that's what I was, suddenly very hungry. I looked out the window; the snow still fell, large flakes and thick. White, everything covered in white.

The quiet, after all our bellowing was peaceful. To make sure the absolute silence would not tempt us to break it, I put on the Mozart String Quintets.

Coffee was a good idea. After it began to perk, I set about preparing a meal of sorts, a plate of cold chicken, sliced tomatoes, potato salad, and other odds and ends.

Why allow him free time, even while I was eating? I got out a card table and placed it directly in front of his head. He watched me as I set it up. On this very special New Year's Eve, a whimsical touch was not beyond me. I put a candle in one of the heavy brass candlesticks, got a small vase, and stripped off one carnation from a bunch in a larger vase.

By the time I sat down, barely two feet in front of him, with my food before me, there was a smirk on his face in acknowledgment of my intent.

I lit the candle, picked up my glass of champagne, and dipped it in a silent toast to him. In return he crossed his eyes at me; he crossed them perfectly. Cross-eyes always make me smile. I couldn't help laughing. After I'd sipped from the glass, he quickly puffed up his cheeks and blew the candle out. Then he turned his head to the side, facing away from me.

This cat was spunky.

I stood, picked up the table and moved it into his line of vision. He didn't budge until I'd moved the chair around and sat down. Then, as I took my first bite, he turned his head the other way, facing the living room. I moved the card table and chair, once more sitting down in front of him. When I began to eat he swiveled his head around again.

"Ah-ah," I said, standing and going after the coffee percolator. "Back this way."

"Jesus!" He glanced at the coffeepot and immediately turned his head, facing the card table. He thought I was threatening to pour hot coffee on him. This hadn't occurred to me. Instead I placed the percolator on the butcher block, only an inch or so away from the back of his head. If he attempted to turn or move at all, he would risk a burn.

"Hot stuff!" I wagged a warning finger at him.

He had no alternative but to watch me now. After several bites, I once again lifted my glass in a silent toast before sipping. Again he crossed his eyes at me.

"You know what I wish?" he asked. "You know what I really wish? I wish I could puke right now."

"Be my guest."

"I really do. I'd give my left nut if I could snap my cookies right in front of you."

"Where there's a will, there's a way," I told him.

"I wish I could."

"Maybe you should take a course. They have courses in almost everything nowadays. You could enroll in Puking One, then if you do well—go on to Puking Two. You might even take your master's."

"Whack-o," he muttered.

"Of course, by then I'd have finished eating, so that would defeat your purpose. But then, looking at it another way, you'd have learned a trade." I paused, chewed on a piece of chicken, then wiped off my mouth. "Something your mother and I had despaired of." I laughed; suddenly we were sitting in Ozzie and Harriet's kitchen, having that mandatory breakfast scene that opens most situation comedy shows.

My last sentence had confused him. All I got by way of response was "Huh?"

"Forget it, dumb-ass!"

"I'd really like a shot at you. Jesus, would I!"

"You had your chance but you muffed it."

"Once more. One time. I'd fuckin' total you!"

"Make up your mind. Do you want to puke or do you want to total me? That's the trouble with you young people today—can't make up your minds. And remember, the decision you make today might affect your entire life." I laughed again; Christ, I was getting silly. "Such as it is," I added.

"I think you're flippin'."

"And aren't you lucky to have a ringside seat?"

"Yeah, my luck. Three lemons—pong, pong, pong!" He continued to watch me while I ate. After a while, he sighed. "Mean. Jesus—*mean!* I never saw nothin' like you for mean. I hadda aunt once used to say, 'Mean as cat's meat.' Well, that fits you, you're fuckin' mean as cat's meat. Eatin' in front of a person. I didn't eat since last night. I'm fuckin' hungry." When I didn't reply, he added: "And speakin' of cat's meat—I'm glad your *fuckin' cat's dead!* Serves you right."

I looked up from my food. "My—what?"

I saw it strike him. "Ahh! Oh, oh Jesus, yeah—!" He broke off laughing. "That's right, you didn't *know*—your fuckin' cat's bought the farm! Hee . . ." He howled with delight.

I stood up, all I could do was look at him.

His laughed turned to a cough. When he was coughed out, he said, with pure glee in his voice: "That's *right*, youse didn't know!"

I stepped toward him. "What do you mean, my cat's dead?"

He flinched. "Wait, I'll tell you! Right after I got here, the ball-breaker flew in. My gun fell outta my pocket when I dropped from the skylight. My mistake was puttin' it down when I was collecting the goodies together. I was standing right next to the bed when I heard the key in the lock so I quick ducked underneath. She was only here a couple of minutes when the phone rang. The cat hospital and—"

"The *cat* hospital?"

He shrugged. "Cat hospital, animal hospital. Whatever. Oh, man, she was upset when she heard. She right away called some guy—Fred, she called him—said the cat had died and maybe they should change their plans on accounta how much you liked the cat, plus the combination her goin' off for New Year's. But she listens to a lot of blah-blah-blah on the other end and says yeah, he's right, she'll meet him in a half hour."

I said nothing. What could I say? I could hardly believe it, yet I knew from the way he'd told it he hadn't made it up.

My cat was dead. Bobby Seale was dead. Jesus, the results were still coming in.

"Yeah," Vito sighed, "I kept waitin' for her to drop it on you. Hmn . . . if you treated your cat the way you treat people, it's probably a good thing. See, what I mean is—I'm *hungry!*"

I turned and walked away from him. For a moment I thought of phoning the vet's but I knew it was true.

"I'm goddamn hungry!" he shouted. I wanted him to be quiet, I was suddenly tired of him, weary of hearing his voice. I also could not absorb this latest.

DON'T TAUNT THE WRETCHED!

He laughed again, to my ears a moronic sort of laugh. He had a habit of diverting his laughter to a high keening "Hee . . ." sound. By doing this he was able to keep the laughter from lodging in his throat and bringing on a fit of coughing.

"Hee . . . !" once more and I knew he was laughing about the cat. I let him laugh himself out. When he finished he was quiet for a short spell, until he shouted once more: "Goddamnit, I'm hungry, even in jail they feed you!"

His persistence got to me, that together with his total joy in delivering the news about Bobby Seale. "Let's see if we can't find something for you!"

He cocked his head as I walked to the refrigerator. "You mean it?"

"Sure, I mean it." I took out a bowl of lime jello with bananas that had overstayed its time. I walked back to him. "Here . . ." I upended the bowl, thumping the top and dumping the congealed mass on top of his head.

"Jesus! Oh, *Jesus!*"

I scooped the rest that clung to the bowl out with my hand and pressed it onto his forehead. "There, take it all!"

"You fuckin' crazy-ass bastard! You *bastard!*"

At first I laughed as he shook his head to rid himself of the globs of green dotted with bananas. He swore all the while. I stepped over to the bureau and picked up Kate's hand mirror; I thought I'd let him have a look at himself. When I walked back to him, the sight wasn't as funny as I'd thought it would be, the green mass dotted with yellow-brown spots sliding from his forehead, down the side of his nose, on down his cheeks and then dropping to the pillow I'd put under his chin. He shook his head, most of it slid off easy enough, but some lodged in his hair. It was supposed to look funny, but it didn't and I was annoyed. And already a bit ashamed.

No use pursuing it. As I turned to walk away and put the mirror back, he spit the words out: "I'm *glad* I ripped you off before. Jesus, am I ever! I'm fuckin' glad I did!" I spun around and faced him. "You heard me, you prick!"

"So you did, didn't you? It *was* you!"

"Goddamn right it was. Twice, scraped you clean twice. And I'd do it again. You miserable—"

"Cretin!" I shouted, throwing the mirror to the floor. The crash of glass brought a cry of fright from him. "There, there goes your *luck*, you crummy little bastard!"

I went to him, grabbing him hard by the collar of his shirt and jerking his head up. "You took my book! What did you do with those pages, all those pages in that box? Oh—you bastard!"

He enjoyed my anguish, so much so that he managed, even with his disadvantage, to feign an air of casualness. "Threw 'em out. I thought there'd be some goodies in there. When I broke it open nothin' but a lot of yellow pages with—oh, yeah, and some dirty pictures!" He laughed his semimoronic laugh. "Those I kept."

To shut him up, I slapped him hard on the side of the head. The elation I felt with that solid connection! A cry and a whimper— delight to hear. I raised my hand again. He cringed, as much as he could in his position. "Worked on that for almost a year and you throw it out. I'll tell you one thing, you won't rob anyone again. Not by the time I get through with you!" I noticed jello on my hand, from slapping him. "Uck!" I wiped it off on his neck.

I was breathing hard from pure rage. I sat down at the card table, looked at my plate, then at him. "You slob! Look at you. You don't have to puke to take my appetite away. Just the sight of you is enough."

"Tough shit! Come on, wipe my head off."

"Wipe your ass!"

"Gladly—on your face!" he said.

I upturned the card table, sending everything flying, dishes, vase, food, candlestick. I screamed at him face-to-face, point blank. "Watch your tongue, you little bastard! *Bastard!* I've had enough of you. No lip, no swearing, none of your smartass cracks. Do you hear me?" At last I saw in his eyes the fear I'd wanted to put there. "Do you?" I repeated.

"Yes." He said it quietly.

No quiet for me. I shouted even louder; the words raked my throat. "*Do you hear me?*"

"Yeah—yes. Come on—take it easy." He ducked his head back away from me.

"And no advice, no take it easy. You're going to learn how to behave. Have you got that straight?"

"Yes."

"Yes, sir! Let's hear it—yes, sir!"

"Yes, sir," he said in a small voice.

The picture of him simply dumping out the pages of my book—where, in an alley, in an ashcan?—kept flashing through my head. "Loud and clear. Yes, sir. Let it echo—*Yes, sir!*"

"Yes, sir!" The attempt at projection caused his voice to break. Then he said, his voice shaky now, very shaky, "Jesus . . ."

I slapped him again. "No swearing! The fucking lowlife scroungy petty little half-assed burglars don't swear! Have you got that straight?"

"Yes."

"Yes—*what?*"

"Yes, sir!"

Blind anger coursed through me. I was short of breath but I could not stop. Like a runner at the end of a big mile, I had to keep moving. I paced back and forth. The thoughts I entertained were murderous. I could tell by the silence he was watching me; I knew I had him frightened. My one solace.

After a long while he spoke, his voice was the essence of tentative. "Listen—I'll, I'll make you a deal."

"Sir!"

"Sir. Listen, I'll—if you let me go, I'll—make it up to you for what I took. I'll—

"How?"

"I'll pay you back—you tell me what—you know, the worth of everything—and I'll get the money and pay you back." I only looked at him. "I swear it."

"How?"

"How? I just told you."

"No, *how will you get the money?* Where will you get the money from?"

"I'll get it, I will, I swear to—"

"The book! Jesus, how could you—the book you can't replace!"

"You don't got a copy?"

"*No, I don't got a copy!*" I was shouting again, shouting so loud his eyes blinked in reaction. "Okay, so—so I just tell you the value of everything else. I give you the figure and let you go. I sit here in the lotus position and you'll come trotting back wagging your tail like a good dog—with the money?"

"I swear it, on my mother's grave!"

His attempt to con me doubled my anger. "You take me for a goddamn moron! *Do you?* You rob me twice and now you have the nerve to make me out a fucking idiot?"

"No, what do you mean?"

"I mean this: Just between you and me, I'd say I'd be tripping over a long white beard if I let you hotfoot it out of here."

"My mother's grave! I'll get the money and pay you back."

"Where would you get it, you keep telling me, but you leave out the *how?*"

"Some I got, I got some."

"Bully. Where do you keep it hidden, under a rock in the backyard? Or sewn up in the lining of your overcoat? Nothing as common as a bank, I take it?"

He slipped into bravado. "Sure, in a bank. Where else?"

"Where else indeed? Especially with all the burglaries nowadays, eh? After all, that's what banks are for. Savings or checking?"

"Huh?"

"Savings or checking account? Do you keep it in a savings or checking account?" When he hesitated, I said, "Or both?"

He took my lead too easily. "Yeah, both. Some in each."

I could see the game coming and I relished it. "Ah, big Diamond Vito Antenucci. *Two* bank accounts—what bank?"

"My bank."

"Your own private bank? The Vito Antenucci Federal Loan and Trust Company?"

"No, come on, the bank I go to."

"But what's the name of this bank?"

"The—ah, the—"

I snapped my fingers. "Quick, the name. Surely you know the name of this great bank where you have your goodies stashed away?"

Bravado again. "Sure I do. What do you think?"

"Well, spit it out, man." I clapped my hands together; he blinked. "The name, the name!"

He cried out now in a husky voice: "You make me nervous—yelling and—"

"Two accounts at a bank and you can't think of the *name* of it!" I reached up and turned on the hanging kitchen light above his head; it shone down upon him. I would play out the game fully, if that's the way he wanted it. He squinted under the glare of the light. "Okay, maybe we can narrow it down. Where is this bank of yours?"

"It's—hey, do we gotta have that light? I still gotta headache."

"Yeah, we gotta. Where is it, the bank?"

"It's—that one up at Radio City."

"Oh, *that* bank, the big one on the corner?"

"Yeah, that one on the corner."

I picked up the pace. "What corner—Fifth or Sixth?" As he opened his mouth, I went on. "Or both?"

"Both?" he asked in confusion. "No, just on one corner."

I sighed. "Thank God! But which one?" He looked dazed. "Hey, Vito-baby, maybe this whole thing would go better if you spoke *Italian*. Is it a language problem?"

A snort from him. "You nuts?"

Despite the coolness of his statement, I could distinguish the perspiration on his forehead from the remains of the jello. "It's your bank, Vito-baby. Christ, man, it's your bank! How do you get your goddamn money in and out if you don't know where it is?"

"I do—but you yell—and I—Honest, you gotta believe me. I got—"

"*You don't got nothing!* You lying little cheating goddamn robbing bastard you! On top of everything else, you lied to me, didn't you?"

"No, I didn't lie."

I grabbed hold of his shirt; buttons popped. "Yes, you did. Admit it, you rotten little crum!"

"Don't hit me, don't hit me." He whined, bit his lip and tried to pull away from me. "Yes . . . okay, lay off—I lied."

"Why? *Why?*"

He shouted back at me; he was close to tears! "Because—to get outta here—because—for the main reason—"

"For the main reason—*what?*"

"You got me spooked."

"Spooked? How spooked?" I asked.

"Forget it, I—forget it."

I grabbed him tighter. "No, we won't forget it. Spooked, how come spooked?"

"I don't know, but—looks like you got some, like some big hassles and maybe you're not in such a good mood."

I laughed. "You sure have a way with words. But why do I spook you?"

"For the main reason—I don't know what you got in your head."

"And that scares you?" I asked.

"Yes."

I let go of him. His fright exhilarated me. "Good! Jesus, how great! The way I feel tonight, I spook myself. I never scared anyone in my life. Maybe my luck's changing. I'll tell you one thing. I'm *glad* I scare you. And before I'm through with you, you lying little miserable punk bastard—I'll scare the holy shit out of you."

Although he tried to brave it through with a smile, he spoke on the edge of a whimper. "I can't tell whether you're—"

"What—kidding? You think I'm kidding? Kidding, I am not!"

An involuntary little twitch tugged his mouth down and over to the side. "Jesus, what are you gonna do?"

"I don't know. Oh, but I'll come up with something, don't you worry." I was pacing again. "One thing for sure, Vito-baby—and I give you my word for this, *my mother's grave*—I'll try like hell not to make it boring!"

I continued pacing, could not wind down. Something inside me revved at top speed. His presence, the unadulterated mindlessness of him, kept the desire for revenge burning. More than a desire, a demand payment.

At any rate, I, who have always subscribed to the theory that we homo sapiens are responsible for our actions, unless way the far side of crazy, that is to say certified mad, nothing less than full papers—I could no more have stopped this rush into uncharted behavior than I could have stopped breathing. So I paced, concentrating only upon a suitable and, the devil and my imagination willing, colorful means of retaliation.

"Hey, guy—" I paid him no attention. "Hey, guy, I hate to bring this up, but I gotta take a leak."

"Leak away," I said, without looking at him.

The phone rang. It was Ginny Steeples, the actress Carmine Rivera had mentioned was giving a party. It was to be a costume party, and I was invited.

"Help!" Vito screamed. "HELP!"

"Excuse me," I said to Ginny. I put the phone down and had only to step toward him to silence him. Back on the phone I declined but thanked her. I could hardly wait to hang up.

Crazy Carmine, there was an idea! He was dedicated to sex in all its unusual forms, to hear him and those who knew him tell it. He had tried to snag me for months; failing that, he'd attempted to get me involved in group happenings, the component parts of which he thought might be to my liking. He was so ferociously dedicated to *le sport* that I was put off, made wary and shy.

To all outward appearances completely masculine, he cut a handsome figure: tall, broad-shouldered, narrow-hipped, Spanish, black eyes, extremely fair skin—the shocking contrast—and curly black hair. Aristocratic gypsy, if there be one.

Despite his striking appearance, there was, a fraction of an inch beneath the surface, especially behind the endless black of his eyes, the hint of something extremely freakish. He openly advertised his taste for the bizarre; I'd heard that he was on the S end of S and M. Whatever he did, whatever his inclinations, I had a very strong hunch his tastes were not only bizarre but—dirty. Really dirty. I'd often seen him with hustlers, hookers, outcasts, and other assorted grotesqueries.

The idea of offering my prisoner to him on the sacrificial altar that was my sink, on this special New Year's Eve, was not a bad notion at all. Carmine would find Vito interesting, I was sure of that. Crazy Carmine would provide a lively show at worst; and, at best, perhaps come up with something truly unusual.

Mainly, this rugged little Italian burglar would be soundly humiliated.

(Another thought: Had my curiosity been aroused by Carmine? Was this a chance to investigate his world without becoming personally soiled? No time to dwell on that!)

"Hey!" Vito shouted. "Did youse hear me—I gotta take a leak!"

Ignoring him, I looked up Carmine's number. He lived in the

Village, not far away on Eleventh Street. His weaselish roommate, Sammy, who appeared to be more of a servant of Carmine's, answered.

"Hi, Sammy—Jimmy Zoole. Is Crazy Carmine there?"

"Jimmy Zoole—hi! No, he won't be home for an hour or so, then he's got a slew of parties."

"Ask him to phone me when he comes in, tell him I have something for him."

"—Have something?" I could hear the leer in Sammy's voice. But then Sammy would leer at a deodorant commercial.

"Yes, a person." I looked at Vito, who was paying close attention. "A creature, tell him this creature's ready and waiting. He'll do anything Crazy Carmine wants."

Snicker. "Anything—that's a big order with C. C." Sammy giggled. "You know what C. C.'s—ah, specialty is?"

"Yes, I know all about his specialty. He'll fit right in, don't worry." (I had no idea, this was for Vito's sake.)

"This doesn't sound like Jimmy Zoole—I mean the voice does, but—"

"Well, it is. Have Carmine give me a ring. I think he'll be amused." I gave him my number, wished him Happy New Year, and hung up.

Vito mimicked me: "I think he'll be amused!"

"Yes. I think he will."

A snort from Vito. "Crazy Carmine! That makes two of youse—Crazy Carmine and Crazy Jimmy." Pause. "Crazy Carmine, huh?"

"If you think I'm crazy, wait'll you get a load of Carmine. You'll get a kick out of him."

Vito affected a casual wise-guy tone: "Yeah? Hmn . . . this specialty, what's his specialty?"

Now that I'd set a course of action in motion, I felt frisky again. I knew Carmine would return my call. "Oh, let it be a surprise."

"Who knows, maybe I dig it." Then his laugh, more of a bronchial bark. "Wouldn't that be a bitch! You planning this big scene—

and I dig it! That would really break your balls." Another bark; when he recovered, he slipped back to his casual voice: "Come on, give me a clue?"

I winged it: "Oh, just a little thing he does with figs and mice."

He crossed his eyes. "Figs and *mice*?"

"Yeah, what's the matter, you don't like mice?"

"No, it's the figs that bug me, they give me the shits." A snicker. "Figs and mice! Hey, would you mind takin' this pillow away, it's all cruddy with jello. Might turn your buddy Carmine off."

I got another pillow and replaced the messy one. "Thanks." Then I got a bath towel and wiped the excess jello off his head. He laughed. "Christ, all this treatment, I feel like I been moved into the death house." He looked up at me as I finished cleaning him off. "So . . . what are you gonna do—watch?"

"Wouldn't miss it for the world."

"Too bad I hocked your Polaroid." I let the remark pass. He cleared his throat, then said "Ah . . ." in a most insinuating way, with the intonation of Bugs Bunny before an especially fresh *What's up, Doc?* "Ah . . . what's the matter, you gotta call someone else in to do a man's job?"

I shot him a look. His expression was pure camp, his lips were pursed, even his eyes appeared to be pursed, completely contradicting his former manner. When I only looked at him, because of my surprise, he quickly switched, dropping all camp and speaking in a tough voice, almost a shout: "You heard me, what's the matter, you can't do your own work?"

"I wouldn't touch you with a ten-foot pole."

"So—get a twelve-foot pole." Another laugh-turned-cough. "Hey, you know how to break a Pole's finger? Hit him in the nose!"

"Very funny, you ought to have your own pizza stand."

"Yeah, but first I gotta pee. Honest, I'm tellin' you! Come on, guy!"

"No, I don't have to! You start without me."

"*What?*"

"Go ahead, you're right over the sink."

"Not in my clothes—Jesus!"

I crossed the room and stood in front of him. "You don't think I'm going to let you up, do you? You don't think I'm that stupid?"

"Just while I pee."

"Then what? I suppose you'll come back, lie down, and let me tie you up again?" This was too much even for him to promise; he remained silent. "Well, you win points for not trying to con me into that."

"Come on, guy, I gotta pee!" A pause, then the trace of a whine: "Hey, guy, listen, why do you gotta tie me up anyways?"

I walked away from him. "Let's not get into theory."

"I mean it. We'll turn on, smoke some pot. Oh, I heard when you and the ballbreaker was talkin', but this stuff is guaranteed to turn you on. It's the wildest—Senegalese Thunderfuck, it's called."

"I can turn on without letting you up, you know."

"Yeah—but I gotta get up to pee! Honest to God, my teeth"—pronounced teet—"are startin' to float. Jesus, you're stubborn, stubborn and mean."

"We're none of us perfect. Like I said, you're right over the sink."

His voice broke in disbelief. "In the *sink*! That's dirty!"

I laughed. "It's *my* sink, what do you care?"

"Yeah, and they're *my* clothes, not in my clothes." As I walked to pour myself more champagne, he added: "Okay, at least give me a hand"—a pause for dramatic effect—"take it out for me."

This stopped me. "*Take it out for you?*"

"Yeah, take it out for me." When I didn't reply, he added: "What's the matter, is it a *language* problem?" His voice was coated in sly. "Or—you afraid you might like it?"

I raised a hand and came at him. "You little creep!"

He laughed and cringed at the same time. "Oh-ho, what'd I—hit a nerve? I bet I could show you a good time, too! Go ahead, just take it out for me? Hey, you ever hear this one?

"Take it in your hand, Mrs. Murphy,
It only weighs a quarter of a pound,
It has feathers 'round its neck like a turkey,
You can take it standing up or lyin' down!"

He laughed until he began to cough again.

I could not believe my ears. "Wait a minute—don't tell me you're *queer*, too!"

This suggestion did not rattle him in the least. "What are you—takin' a census?" A beat. "Or—are you interested?"

On top of everything, his presumption, his insinuation, infuriated me. "Hey, remember me! No lip, no back talk, no smartass! You're not the boss here, remember that? You're just a little piece of immobile shit! I asked you a question—are you queer?"

I expected retrenchment from him. Not at all. "Tell you what, why don't you unzip me and take it out. If it starts to grow, you got your answer! Then if *yours* starts to—"

I swung a quick slap to his jaw. "Punk!"

"Jesus, what do you—only like to clout people you got tied up? You really get a kick hittin' on people can't defend themselves?" I walked away from him. "Anybody that uptight's got a problem. And tell me you don't swing both ways! All actors swing, I never met an actor yet didn't swing. Shit, the whole world swings now—if you catch 'em at the right moment. Go ahead, tell me!"

My silence only spurred him on.

"Go ahead, big man, no problem, take it out—it won't bite you!" Another of his moronic laughs. "What—you think it's got teeth?" Then a switch of tone, the voice strong and angrily insistent. "Come on, goddamnit, let me up! I gotta piss and I'm too old to start wettin' my goddamn pants!"

I did get a kick out of his change of pace, also his chutzpah. Ten minutes earlier he'd been cringing, close to tears. Now that he was creeping into what seemed to be familiar sexual territory, he was cocky and sure of himself.

I glanced out of the window. How thick the snow was falling. It was unreal. As if it were somehow a cover-up for this unreal scene inside my apartment. As long as it fell, I was safe, the charade could continue. I realized this made no sense. But then, *nothing* was making much sense.

"Come on, I don't want to wet myself!"

"I guess you're right. That would be messy, wouldn't it? Well, let's see—" I went to my rolltop desk and rummaged through the cubbyholes. "We can probably come up with an alternative."

"How do you mean?"

"For the main reason—I can't really let you up. Not yet. We've got the whole New Year's Eve ahead of us." I found a pair of large scissors. "Here we go."

Why, I wondered, was I feeling so suddenly buoyant, as if some manner of happy-time spansule had gone off. Was I, in some abstruse way, slipping? Slipping into flipping?

"Whatcha gonna do?" Vito asked, not being able to see the desk from his vantage point.

I walked behind him to where his feet stuck out over the edge of the butcher block. "Let it be a surprise!"

"Surprises again. You musta got bit by a surprise when you was a kid." He craned his neck around as I took the cuff of his pants in one hand and prepared to cut with the other. "Jesus, no! Hey! No—my good pants! I don't have to go! Honest, I don't. Truth! I made it up. I just said that to—"

But I was already cutting up through one cuff.

He did his best to twist and squirm. "You nut, you fuckin' crazy nut!"

"Watch it, or I'll cut more than just your pants."

"Come on," he whined, "that ain't *funny*! My good pants! How am I supposed to get home?"

I was cutting easily up the back of the leg now. "Who said anything about going home? Some people have a dog, some have a pet cat. My cat's dead—so I got me a pet Vito."

I carried on a conversation with myself as I sliced up his pants legs: "Oh, you have a pet Vito? They're rare, aren't they?"

"Rare? You can't hardly get them no more!"

"Where'd you get your Vito—at the Vito store?"

"No, by God, I found mine right under the bed."

"Under the bed?"

"Yes, Vitos are a lot like cats that way. They adopt *you*, you don't adopt *them*!"

"What about housebreaking?"

I laughed at myself. "Oh, yeah, they housebreak. I'm training mine to go in the *kitchen sink*!"

I'd cut up one leg to the seat, now I began on the other.

"Oh, boy, did the ballbreaker ever have you wrong! You're whacked out of your zook! Jesus, my good pants!"

"No problem for a man of your means, just waltz up to Rockefeller Center and take some money out of either one of your big bank accounts."

In mimicry of my rambling, he executed a rapid-fire series of: "Blah-blah-blah-blah-blah-blah-blah-blah-blah—" ending up with a loud Bronx cheer.

Soon I'd cut up both legs and had only to join the two cuts at the seat of the pants in order to pull them off. As I sliced toward the center. I noticed his shorts, a fancy paisley pattern of the jockey type. "Hey, what nifty shorts, very jazzy, very natty."

A snotty reply. "Those ain't shorts—I got my ass tattooed." He exhaled a long sigh. "Jesus, my good pants. Mean, boy, you really are mean!"

"Mean? You rob me twice, throw away two hundred and twelve pages of a novel, without even thinking, you come back to rob me again—and *I'm* mean!"

"Yeah, mean as cat's meat. I may be all that and more, but at least I ain't mean like you!"

"I'd say your frame of reference is somewhat removed from life as we know it on this planet."

"Get the big Pants Cutter—no shit!"

"No shit! *Voilà*, now you see 'em, now you don't!" I yanked his pants off.

"Jesus!"

I cut down the back of his jockey shorts. "Another snip or two and you're free as a bird."

"Hey!"

"Steady as she goes, we're getting down to the nitty-gritty." The shorts were cut in two. I snatched them off with a flourish. Except for his socks and shirt, which I'd pulled up during the cutting, he was bare.

"This is the capper, runnin' into you. Boy, you really cop the fruitcake for cuckoo!"

He had a rugged build, sturdy legs and small firm but rounded buttocks. They stood up a bit. I thought of Pete, who had said: "I'm an ass man for men and thighs and tits for women. Conversely, I don't like tits on men and I don't much care for women's asses. Give me a good *solid* ass!"

Vito glanced behind him, then up at me. "How do you like the act so far? Nice smile, no teeth, huh?" As I started to walk away from him, he said, "Hey, you like fruit? Take a bite of my ass, it's a peach!"

The music had stopped; I went to turn the records over. "Shut up and piss!"

"I told you, I don't have to."

"Fake it."

"You're very vivid. You're a very vivid person." He sighed. "Okay, what next—nutsy?"

I walked back to the kitchen to get my glass. What an odd word for him to use: *vivid*. Looking at him, the way his shirt was hiked up, his nudity, ankles tied, wrists bound behind him, it all made him look so completely vulnerable, I felt a moment of compassion for him.

As if he could read this, he said, "I know it's dumb to ask, but—could I have a cigarette?"

He could have been trussed up awaiting the guillotine or the firing squad. The simplicity of the request got to me. Also, his resignation, he did seem resigned to his predicament. "Sure, why not?"

"I could?"

"Sure, what the hell, it's New Year's." I walked to the small pile of things I'd taken from his pockets, got a cigarette, lighted it, then went to him and put it in his mouth. He dragged deeply, I took the cigarette out, he exhaled and said, "Thanks, take one."

"I gave it up." He laughed, coughing up the last bit of smoke. "What's so funny?" I asked.

"Kills me," he said. "He beats people up, knocks them the fuck out, ties them up, cuts their clothes off them—but he doesn't smoke. Oh, no, nothin' like *that*."

I smiled at the way he put it.

"Another," he said. I put the cigarette back in his mouth. He took another drag, exhaled, then fell into a fit of coughing.

"You ought to get a room," I told him, as he hacked away.

I didn't even hear the door open, only heard my name. "Jim . . . ?"

We both turned, just in time to see Kate's head peek in the door. If she was surprised, too surprised to speak at first, so was I. I had certainly not expected to see her.

She'd stepped into the room now and was focusing on the strange tableau we must have presented, to the background music of the Mozart String Quintets: the prone figure of Vito, tied down, bare-assed as a babe, yet cynically wise of face, me standing attendance, inserting the cigarette for him to puff, then taking it away as he exhaled. For what seemed ages the only sound in the room was the music.

The expression on her face was priceless. Her eyes mirrored her speechlessness. Yes, for once Kate was speechless.

I glanced down at Vito. His eyes flicked from Kate to me. There was a twinkle, an immediate spark between us.

Kate took another tentative step into the room. For several more seconds no one spoke. Her expression, the complete dumbfoundedness of it, sent my spirits skyrocketing. There was an impulse to laugh, but I didn't want to shatter the cool everyday casualness of mood we'd somehow been caught in.

"Come on in," I said. She stayed where she was. "What a surprise!"

"Surprise . . . ?" she echoed. Her eyes were all pupil. "Jim, what's the—what—"

"I had no idea you'd be dropping by." I stuck the cigarette back in Vito's mouth. "Did you, Vito?"

When I removed it, he spoke on the exhale in an entirely offhand manner: "Uh-uh, no, she didn't say nothin' to me."

"Come on in, make yourself at home." Kate took a few steps farther into the room. "Where's your date?" I asked. Kate did not reply; she could only stare at Vito. "I thought you were off for parties and skiing and things?" Pause. "Kate?"

Her eyes blinked, then flicked to me. "We, ah—were, I mean, we *are*, but—"

"Where is he?"

"Down in the car." She cleared her throat. "But when I called up I got—I mean, I could hear yelling and I got worried."

"Oh, yeah, that . . ."

"Oh, yeah, *that?*" she snapped. She was getting her tongue back. "Jim, what is this? You said—a burglar?"

I glanced down at Vito; he surprised me by winking up at me. I looked back to Kate, I could tell by her expression she'd seen the wink. "Well, more a burglar-friend, burglar-buddy." I took a breath. "—Pal," I added.

I'd had trouble finishing the sentence. Vito giggled. I grinned, too. This did nothing to clear things up for Kate.

"But naked . . . ?"

"Oh, that," I said. "Well, ah—"

I don't know what I would have said if Vito hadn't cut in with: "That's where the buddy part comes in!"

"Yes," I was quick to confirm, then get on with it. "Say, why don't you ask your friend up for a glass of champagne? No hard feelings."

Vito's tone was slyly wise and full of innuendo. "Yeah, ask him up. Maybe we can, you know—all have a little *party?*"

Kate retreated a small step. "No, I don't think—"

"Ah, come on," Vito urged, "it's New Year's Eve." Then the capper: "Is he—humpy?"

"*What?*" Kate asked.

I walked toward the large front windows. "I'll call down, what's his name?"

"No, Jim—don't. He wouldn't—no, please, don't!"

"Okay, whatever you say." The similarity between Vito and Kate struck me. "Hey, you two have the same eyes, you know that?"

She did not react to this; instead a large grin spread over her face. "Jim . . . ?"

"Yes?" I did not permit my grin to show.

"Did you—well, you know, *stage* this? Did you?"

"*Stage* it?" I asked.

"Yes." She took several steps toward me. "Come on, what's going on? I don't get it."

Vito cut in, asking the question in all seriousness. "What—you didn't know he swung both ways?"

Kate's eyes flashed. "I wasn't talking to you!"

He was not intimidated. "But I'm talkin' to *you!*"

I laughed. Kate's eyes snapped at me; clearly said: Stop it!

Vito continued. "Or did you think you was the only one gettin' in on those great—Hugglebunnyburgers?" Oh, the expression on her face when he dropped that phrase! She immediately looked at me, mouth open. I had the idea she was about to speak, but Vito went on: "We call ours Bang-arama-thons, but what's the diff? Bang-arama-thons—Hugglebunnyburgers, six of one, half dozen of the other. What you lose on the peanuts, you make up on the bananas, right?"

This small aria from Vito had completely thrown her. She looked at me again. "Ah . . ." was the sound she uttered. I gave her a helpless little shrug, as if to say: "*Well, listen . . .*" I could see words and anger forming up. "Jim, what's the explanation for—"

But Vito was still on. "Thought you had him half figured out, didn't you?"

"I'm not talking to you!" she once again advised him.

"But I'm talkin' to you, Miss Freight Train. You're so curious about the scene here, I'll lay it out for you."

His attack gave every promise that he would. I could tell by her expression that although she had marked him rotten, she was not beyond receiving information from the enemy. That is, as long as I remained mute. As for me, I could hardly wait to hear his explanation.

"You think he's square, huh? Let me stuff your ears. We been makin' it since last August twenty-second, off and on." (I tried to

hide my amazement; where did he get *that* date?) Vito picked up
on her look of pure incredulity. "Oh, not steady like you. But we
racked up some vivid one-nighters. Beautiful, really, I mean he really
knows how to toss the old salad. So tonight—"

We heard a knock on the door, which Kate had left cracked open
an inch or so. We all looked in that direction.

"Kate? Jesus, what a building, no lights in the hall, no one else—"
With that he was inside the door. "This building's really weird."

I thought: Wait until you get a look at the kitchen, buddy.

Kate pulled herself together instantly. "Oh, Fred, I was just about
to come down. Ah—Jim, this is Fred Gable. Fred—Jim."

I'd stepped away from Vito, by now, and was between him and
this Fred. "Hi, good to meet you." I walked to him and we shook
hands. "Same here," he said.

Fred Gable was my height, good-looking, around thirty-five,
wearing a smart overcoat, a dark suit, wide far-out tie, hair longish,
styled. Total appearance: with it. But I had a feeling he was with it
because that was the current mode, not because it came natural to
him. Actually, he looked like a sixties ad-agency man dressed up for
the seventies.

He had been concentrating upon me as fully as I had upon him
and had not yet spotted Vito. I stepped to the side and stretched
an arm out toward the kitchen. "And—I'd like you to meet Vito,
Vito Antenucci." As the sight of Vito registered solidly upon Fred,
I added, "Excuse him, he can't shake hands right now."

Fred did not utter a word, only looked for a long moment at
Vito, then quickly to Kate; I suppose for a comment of some sort.
When it was obvious he would get none from her, he returned his
attention to Vito. Vito regarded Fred for a long appraising moment,
then turned to Kate. "Hum-pee!" He pulled a quick switch and
addressed Fred in a regular-guy tone: "Hi, Fred, how's it hanging—
loose?"

Words did not come easily to anyone, except Vito. There was a
lengthy silence, beyond which it would have been uncomfortable to

stretch. Suddenly I thought of the cat. "Kate, why didn't you tell me about Bobby Seale?"

She addressed me out of habit, "Oh, darling—I was going to, but I couldn't, not leaving the note and—I felt so bad. Didn't I, Fred?" (Fred's eyes were still aimed at Vito) "And with New Year's and all, I figured you'd find out soon enough. I'm so sorry! I know I didn't like him, but—I'm sorry, Jim."

Silence again. I was the host, so I broke it. "What about a New Year's drink. Fred?"

Kate cut in immediately. "Oh, we'd better be running." She glanced at her watch. "It's late, I just wanted to stop by and—"

"Oh, come on," Vito said. "Stick around—we'll plug an onion!"

I laughed. Even Kate emitted a small nervous laugh before saying, "Well—"

"You think that's funny?" Fred asked her.

"What—*that?*" she asked, indicating Vito.

"No—'stick around, we'll plug an onion'?" Before she could reply, he gestured toward Vito and spoke with a feigned casualness that told me he was going to play the Vito question extremely cool. "But while we're at it—what is *that?*"

"Well—" was all Kate could summon.

I cut in; I know it was cheap but I received a brief mental flash of that square handsome face with the long hair laboring horizontally over Kate and I was instantly jealous. "Oh, I thought I introduced you. Vito Antenucci, Fred—ah—Garble."

"Gable," he corrected.

To my surprise, Kate, who was not a giggler, giggled again. Now Fred shot her a look. The look had its effect, forcing her into another "Well—"

"All you do is sigh and say, 'Well—' "

"Really?" she asked. She shrugged, then added: "Well—" A hand flew up to her chest. "Oh, Christ, I did it again!" I could see her self-annoyance at that. "So—it's New Year's, so I guess I can sigh and say 'well' if I want to."

I had no idea where we were going from here on in. Fred glanced around at each of us in turn. He settled on me. With a smile, he said, "Okay, let's level. What's the bit? I've got a sense of humor, too."

Vito to the rescue: "You ain't racked up any weepers so far. 'Cept for your name!"

"Oh, Fred, can't you take a joke!" (Hah—Kate was not about to confess to *not* knowing!)

This whole confrontation was tilting so, I simply went with an impulse. Walking to the dartboard on the wall next to the bookcase, I picked off two darts. "Didn't Kate tell you about our games? Now—*no fair throwing them straight at him!* You have to lob them up in the air." Holding out the darts, I walked to Fred. "Try a few?"

"Yeah," Vito said, "hit my ass and win a Cadillac!"

Fred snorted, waved me away, and turned to Kate. "Kate, how's about it? Would you mind letting me in on the gag?"

"Oh, Fred, don't be such a stick. It's just—New Year's Eve, for heaven's sake."

"You keep saying that. I know it's New Year's Eve. If you say it one more time—" Fred's cool was blown. "Oh, hell, I mean I understand freaky, but"—this to Kate—"I'm asking you one last time. You know him, what's the—"

Kate finally leveled in full exasperation: "Frankly, I haven't a clue. I don't know! Let's get out of here!"

Now it was Fred who laughed. "That's the first time I ever heard you admit you didn't know anything."

I laughed with him; he'd caught on to her fast.

Fred regarded me. "Sweet and awfully dear, you said." He turned to Kate. "If this is your idea of sweet and dear, we're in for one helluva weekend. Come on." He walked quickly to the door. "Good luck, gentlemen—whatever it is you do."

He stepped out into the hall.

Kate's eyes narrowed as she hissed at me. "What are you *up to?* You make me look like a stupid—"

"Kate, come on!" His voice from the stairs.

As she walked toward the door, she threw a parting shot at Vito. "I hope he scores a bull's-eye!"

Vito shot back: "So do I, Angel-tits!"

A final gasp of annoyance from her and she was gone. Vito and I broke up. Easy laughter at first, but soon we were howling. His laugh, as usual, converted to a fit of coughing. When he was able to control himself, he said, "Blew her mind! We blew her stack! We didn't do nothin' to clear Old Fred's up either."

I staggered over to him. "Bang-arama-thon!" I roared, slapping him on the rump. This set us off again. I was surprised and delighted with his performance. "I never saw her so—She's always so Holy Rock-of-Gibraltar-sure-of-herself! August twenty-second! Where'd you snatch that from? And 'Stick around—we'll plug an onion'? "

"August twenty-second, my birthday, the last day of Leo. See, I used to be a chronic liar." (That killed me, spoken like: I used to be a rug salesman.) "And I learned, if you hit people right off with the specifics of the issue, they swallow it. See, when I said August twenty-second, I'll bet right away she's thinking: Jesus, he's got the date and everything. And probably she was trying to think back to August—did I see him a lot in August, every night, or what?" He laughed. "I snatch 'em from the air, you get good at it. 'Stick around—we'll plug an onion'—that's from an old friend of mine, Jitters. Old Jitters ate it."

"Ate it?"

"Yeah, died, he died."

Now this is where Vito made his mistake.

He took a deep breath, sighed, and said, rather ordered: "Come on, get these straps off me, this position is a bitch!" When I only looked at him, he said: "Come on!"

"Pardon?"

"Come on, let me the fuck up!" Bad timing, he was jumping the gun.

"How's that?"

"I get to get up now!"

Very bad, he was telling me, not asking. *"No comprendo,"* I said.

"What! Come on, you gotta, now you gotta!"

"No, I don't *gotta.*"

"Yeah—you do! Sure, you do. After what I—"

"Not on your life!"

"But why—*Jesus!*"

"Why—for the main reason, I'm starting to have one helluva time!"

"Yeah? Good for you—you turd!"

"Watch it, Vito! You think just because we put one over on the ballbreaker, that settles the score? Let me tell you something—"

"First, I'll tell *you* something! You're an A-Number-One Prick! Yeah, an' without the catsup!"

"Listen, you ignorant little wop bastard, I worked for ten months on those pages, ten months of grinding goddamn hard brain-bending work. And you come along and throw it out with the *trash?* You think a little joke like you pulled makes up for that?"

Now the unattractive whine crept into his voice. "Jeez, but—you wrote it once, you could write it again, couldn't you?"

"It's harder to *remember* what you wrote than writing it down originally. I've already spent that first creative—Oh, shit, you wouldn't know what I'm *talking* about. Anyhow, I can't just sit here all day on a velvet cushion writing it all over, then have the servants fix dinner. I have to look for work."

"What about this aunt of yours? One she was blah-blahing about, this—Claire?"

"What about her? What are *you* all of a sudden—a social case-worker?"

"I'm just tryin' to help."

I had to laugh. "Help!"

"Yeah, what's so funny?" he asked.

"You! Jesus, I've had enough help from you. That's why I've got you tied up. I don't want any more help from you."

"Okay, now let me tell you something. You keep this up and I'll get you for it—if it's the last thing I do."

"Don't threaten me," I told him.

"Fuck you and the horse you rode in on! This friend of mine, Jitters, one used to say, 'Stick around, we'll plug an onion.' Jitters was a Jew and you know what else he used to say? Ga-noog is ga-noog! You know what ga-noog means? It means enough. Like enough is enough! Comes a time when you've had your kicks with me and then, baby, ga-noog is ga-noog! You stash that away in your attic—and remember it!"

His nerve in threatening me did not sit well. "No threats from you—crum! A crum doesn't make threats!"

"That's another thing. You can call me a lot of things—but crum isn't one of them! Another thing you oughta know—"

"Tell me, O Oracle! Lay it on me, Vito-baby!"

"You mortify a person and a person doesn't forget that. You can do a lot of things to a person, but when you mortify him, he doesn't forget! And just remember, you gotta let me up sometime and then—watch out, Jimmy-baby! 'Cause I'll fix your ass good! You broken-down excuse for a flop actor!"

I slapped him hard. "Don't *threaten* me—you crum!"

"Ga-noog, you bastard!" He screamed until his neck muscles bulged. "You bastard—goddamnit—*ga-noog!*"

I felt angry and bullyish and dirty and—in seconds—tired and deeply depressed again.

What I wanted to feel was—reckless.

What I did not want to do was bungle my catch.

The elation I'd felt when Kate was there, only minutes before, had vanished. Most frustrating of all was the admission that I had not the slightest *practical* idea what to do with this Vito Antenucci.

Even the notion of Carmine now appeared a slight conceit. There would be no relief in turning him over to the police; this had never once occurred to me as the end solution. Obviously I could not kill him, nor could I picture myself engaging in serious torture.

Unless—and for a moment I wished this—he had not thrown out my pages, but rather had deposited them in some specific place and would not, for whatever reason, divulge it. Then I could set to work with imagination and relish to pry the information from him. But this was a daydream, having no basis in fact.

I could not simply let him go; the very thought carried a disturbing undertone. I was, I had to admit, uneasy, about the possibility of retaliation. He had come up, so far, with more than his share of surprises. I did not really know what to make of this character.

What a fizzle this could be, more than a fizzle, a *failure*. The word gave me the shivers. I was sinking; my spirits were sagging.

Energy was what I needed.

I walked to the bathroom and opened the cabinet. Kate was disposed, at times, to taking Dexamyl for a pickup on long photographic assignments. There on the top shelf was the vial, half filled with the small fat green vaguely heart-shaped Dexamyl. I usually avoided anything stronger than aspirin, but Kate had once prevailed upon me to take a Dexi to calm my nerves for a musical audition that had got me particularly rattled. It had produced the desired effects: I felt well liked, talented, all in all filled with general euphoria.

Euphoria was called for now. I quickly filled a glass of water and gulped one down.

When I walked out of the bathroom, Vito Antenucci said, in a low, barely audible voice: "Could I have a glass of water, please?"

The seriousness of the request, the simplicity, and the addition of "please" got to me.

"Sure." I walked to the sink, ran a glass of water, stepped in front of him, and tilted it to his mouth.

He kept his eyes full on me all the while he sipped. To my considerable annoyance I found myself glancing away from him. "Thanks," he said when he'd finished.

"More?" I looked at him; his gaze was still fastened on me.

"No." He blinked his eyes, then spoke in the same understated seriousness of tone he'd used when asking for water. "So—what next?"

I walked away from him, feeling impotent and embarrassed and still dog-tired and aware it would take a good half hour for the pill to work. I felt vulnerable in his presence without energy, also without an answer to his question. I grabbed my overcoat and gloves, snatched up my muffler and a pair of galoshes, and left the apartment, locking the door behind me. He did not make a sound. I'd been so anxious to get away from the coolness of his look that I sat down on the top step of the landing to slip on my galoshes.

A while later I sat on a concrete stub, part of a dilapidated wharf at the edge of the Hudson River. Electric bulbs across in Jersey flashed 11:04.

The snow still fell, thick heavy flakes straight down. I watched as they plopped into the shiny vinyl black of the river and became part of it. Despite the heavy snowfall, the complete windlessness of the night prevented the air from being unbearably cold.

Even so, a triple shiver crawled up my back and arms. I could feel the flesh wrinkle. An entire squad of men walked over my grave. After the spasm I sat gazing numbly out over the river.

Now, I had my first quiet moments over the passing of Bobby Seale. *Bobby, why didn't you tell me you were sick before it was too late? Bobby Seale, I will miss the holy hell out of you!*

His death, on top of the rest, was an extremely bad joke.

Were there creatures hatched upon this planet and soundly stamped *Born Losers!* Unreturnable, nonrescindable.

Was I one of them?

Can the pure will to succeed, can this be used to pole out of the quagmire?

How much of what we are or become depends upon talent, luck, appearance, type, environment, fate, timing, inheritance, intelligence—native or acquired?—or is a lot of it just plain push-and-shove?

Or is it, could it possibly be all predestined? Could we be merely hapless chessmen jerking convulsively through our moves from square to square, helpless to avoid this pitfall, that snare or—yes, sometimes Coming Up Roses, called achievement *and* happiness. Well, relative happiness.

I sat on the concrete stump, collecting snow atop my dome, benumbed and befucked by my colossal overpowering lack of knowledge. Of philosophy, a philosophy of life, of why we're here. Jesus, thirty-eight (Yes, Kate.) And I really had no idea how it all worked, what it was all about.

Did anyone? Yes, I was certain some did. But who? Only the elite?

Don't ask where the names came from. Kenneth Galbraith? Lionel Trilling? Shirley Chisholm? Laurence Olivier? Margaret Mead?

Achievement, they certainly had managed that. But were even *they* relatively happy or were they, deep down underneath it all, as I seemed to be, relatively miserable?

They? They were celebrities. Were there ordinary mortals, more or less simple folk, who felt their own sense of achievement, no matter how small, *and* relative happiness?

Pete Williams. He was relatively the happiest, freest human I'd encountered. Still, a most complex creature. Candid, the most candid person I'd known, but with the happy faculty of leveling with his fellow men without being hurtful. Took joy, inhaled joy from every possible moment of the waking day. And reminded himself of the happiness to be extracted, savored it, and reminded those around him. Played the bad times as lightly as possible, skimmed them, unless there was something to be done about them.

Yes, Pete Williams was certainly relatively happy and he was productive, on his way up.

But look what happened to him, a heart attack at thirty-seven, sitting in a tacky theater on Forty-second Street watching a double feature!

For my added depression, I played a few companion scenes to go with his death. My mother, her liver squirting poison through her system, down to 107 pounds, until all that was left was an enormous pair of eyes that seemed to say: Oh, God, I think this is it, while the tiny skeletal fingers still reached for whatever she could lay her hands on: vodka, gin, wine, whatever she could coax anyone to sneak in to her. Then, toward the end, when I'd paid a surprise visit and found scotch in her ginger ale and had started to take it away, she said—and she never swore, never got really drunk, just saturated ladylike—she said: "Oh, Christ, Jimmy—isn't it late for that?" Then, speaking of herself in the third person, she added: "Look at her, let her have it!" And I did, of course.

I played her death, then her funeral, went back to Pete's funeral, and ticked off several other episodes, now working my way into scenes of personal mortification.

Vignette: Reading for a cigarette commercial, the year before they were banned, at Young & Rubicam. Standing in front of twelve men and three women, ceremoniously seated at an oblong conference table. The expressions on their faces indicated they might have been given the Middle East problem to solve, instead of the selection of one man to smoke a cigarette.

The director, a young smartass, started off by posing this question, "Are you a professional actor?"

"Yes." When what I wanted to say was: *No, I just wandered in off the street, saw the crowd in the waiting room* (there were at least fifty actors jammed into it and strung out along every possible corridor) *and thought maybe I could peddle some dirty postcards. OF COURSE I'm a professional actor, how did you think my name got on your list?*

Next question: "Ever done anything?"

No, I'm a professional actor who hasn't done anything. Instead, another bland "Yes."

"Like what?" he asked, now shuffling lists about on the table in front of him. Obviously this character thought actors were the dreck of the earth. "Like what?" he repeated, now glancing up at me.

Like bury my foot up to the heel in your ass! But I dutifully rattled off a list of credits.

On it went, the rudeness piling up in burning layers until I'd passed the point at which I should have called a screeching halt. Finally he said, "Okay, I guess you're an actor, all right." (Hey, Maw, I passed the quiz!) "Now this is what we're looking for. Oh, do you swim?"

"Yes."

"Good, let's see how good." He glanced at the others round the table and grinned as if it were a joke. Most of them grinned back. "Now, you dive in and take a swim around. It's a good brisk morning swim, invigorating, really great. You climb out of the pool, just kinda leap out of it, shake off the water, light up a cigarette—there's a pack and matches on the sofa there—our new *Okay* brand. Take a good long drag, look at the cigarette, cock your head and say, 'Okay! What a way to start the day!' Simple as that." He glanced around the group once more, smacked his hand down on the table, and said, "Dive in, go to it!"

"Dive in?" I asked.

"Dive right in!" He saw the expression on my face. "What's the matter—you know how to pantomime, don't you?"

"Sure."

"Go to it then!"

He leaned forward in anticipation of this great aquatic event, as did most of the others.

Feeling completely landlocked, beached, in fact, I glanced around the room. Oh, well, play the game. I walked to the leather sofa, slipped off my loafers, and stepped up on it.

"Oh, please—not on the sofa!" One of the women, a scrawny little sparrow type with feather bangs, stood up, one hand to her tiny breasts.

"Sorry." I got off. It would have been nice to have had a little make-believe leverage at the very least. Instead, standing on the thick carpet in my stocking feet, pants, shirt, tie, and jacket, I dived in, swam the length of the conference table, halfway back again, pantomimed out, and shook off the water. I was about to pick up the pack of cigarettes when the director said, "You didn't seem to be enjoying the swim."

No, I didn't, you see I was trying to avoid a little speck of shit floating in the pool—you!

But, oh no, Y & R make their share of commercials and word

gets around. I gagged back my pride, choked on it and uttered a stupid, "Oh?"

"No, try to give us the feeling you're really *digging* it. Enthusiasm, that's what we're looking for. Try it again."

So, this thirty-six-year-old—at that time—man dived in again, made some feeble attempts at Ah'ing and Oh'ing and other happy water sounds, plastered a frozen grin upon his face, leapt out of the nonexistent pool, picked up the cigarettes and—his hand was *shaking in rage*, shaking so much he could barely connect the flame to the tip of the cigarette. The sight of my trembling fingers threw me completely, so much that I forgot what the line was. "Sorry, what was the line?"

The director's face stretched to a smirk. "Do you always shake like that?" Mr. Sensitivity, he.

"No," I said, attempting a last-minute save, "only when provoked." Oh, how lame!

Crimson-faced, not looking at anything except my loafers, I picked them up and left the room as quickly as I could.

Sitting on the concrete stub, as I began to indulge in yet another dark-brown vignette, this one played out at my local unemployment office—Yes, *thir*, Christ, I got a million of 'em!—it occurred to me I was doing everything in my power to sabotage the Dexamyl.

I stood, reached up, and touched the fingers of my hand to the top of my head. A good inch or so of spongy snow had settled there. I shook it off, shaking myself out of the unemployment office at the same time.

No, this was not on course toward the mood I'd hoped for. I glanced across the river: seventeen minutes to twelve.

Seventeen minutes to New Year's. I stamped my feet hard to rid them of the caked snow. This triggered a flow of energy. Stepping off from the wharf, I could feel those tiny shakes just beginning to percolate in my stomach.

A figure, one of the habitual cruisers self-assigned to that area, stepped out from the side of a parked truck. "Hey, buddy, how about going for a beer?"

"Got to get home for New Year's!" My voice came out loud and cheery and sounded as if I meant it. I did. I had company and I had to get home for New Year's. I headed east under the West Side Highway. As I walked I ran through a brief dossier of negative-positives: I was not crippled, I had my health, my hair, my virility, I was not destitute, I might not be a brilliant actor, but I was a good one, I did have a book to write, a book I knew I *could* write, so I was thirty-eight, not exactly a geriatrics case.

My feet went out from under me for a second. I skidded, slipped and regained my balance without falling. I heard myself laugh.

I thought of Kate and laughed even more. Knowing her curiosity, I was certain she would not be able to shake the scene she'd witnessed out of her mind. It would be driving her around in maddening circles. It would color her entire New Year's and undoubtedly stain a few days after.

I thought of Pete again. Pete, who would often begin a phone conversation with: "Had any adventures?"

I was certainly slam-bang in the middle of an adventure, that was a nonvariable, that was for damned sure. I had actually caught and overpowered the rotten little punk burglar who'd robbed me twice and was attempting to make it an even three. Pete would have been proud of me.

It wasn't until I reached my block that an uneasy thought occurred to me: What if he'd somehow got loose? My heartbeat quickened. Why the hell had I left him there alone? *Alone?* Could I have gotten a burglar-sitter? I laughed again, but hurried toward my building.

My fears increased as I put the key in the downstairs lock. I ran up the stairs, unlocked the front door, and stepped into the room. I was short of breath.

He was there, as he'd been before. He read the reason for my breathlessness and laughed. I closed the door without locking it. The sight of him bucked me up.

Now only nine minutes to midnight. I swung into action, first moving the TV set onto a hassock directly in front of him, then dragging up an easy chair for myself and placing it next to the sink unit, so we would both have a view. I got out the paper hats and horns I'd bought for Claire. "Might as well do it up right, don't you think?"

No reply, I picked out a purple-and-silver pointed hat and was about to put it on him when I noticed a few smattering remains of the jello. I got the bath towel I'd used before, dampened it, and cleaned off his forehead and hair as best I could. He did not look at me or even indicate his feelings at being tidied up. I put the hat on him, slipping the elastic strap under his chin. He did nothing to help and because of his prone position, the hat ended up pointing straight ahead of him. I slipped it back, so it stood up perpendicular. "There, that's a bit jauntier." I stepped away from a measured look at him. "Hmn, still you don't look all that—there's a touch missing. Would you like your horn now?" Silence. "No? All right, we have—ah, not even five minutes to go. Can you stand the suspense?"

I turned the TV set on, switching channels until I found a live broadcast from the Taft Hotel. The cameras cut from the girl band singer, bouncing her way through "These Are a Few of My Favorite Things," to the mostly middle-aged couples who jostled each other about on the dance floor. I opened another bottle of champagne, poured myself a glass, then got a small saucer and filled it, placing it on the sink in front of his chin.

"For New Year's you might as well have your own saucer of champagne. That way you won't have to depend upon me—in case I get carried away with the festivities." He only stared at it. "There you go, lap it up, there's more where that came from." He turned his head to the side, away from me. "I hope you're not going to sulk! Are you going to sulk?"

I snatched up the belt I'd taken from around his waist and smacked him on the ass, not especially hard, but enough to produce a smart sound. He winced in surprise only, but did not cry out. His silence infuriated me. I raised the belt again. But I was shocked enough by what I'd done so that I dropped it. "Go ahead and sulk then!"

I put on my paper hat, picked up my champagne, and sipped it. Vito was motionless. "Playing dead dog?" I asked. No reply. I picked up a horn and tooted it in his ear. This caught him by surprise. His body jerked and he stifled a small cry. "Oh, there's life in the old crum yet!"

I sat down, took another long drink, and sighed: "Jesus, I can't wait to see what they have lined up for me in the *new* year!"

The singer ended her number to a messy smatter of applause

and the bandleader, a cross between Vincent Lopez and Lawrence Welk, told us what a great time they were all having "at the Taft Hotel right here in the heart of midtown Manhattan." He wagged his baton and the band launched into "I Want to Be Happy." I glanced at Vito; he was having none of it. The cameras panned over the dancing couples, most of whom looked about as happy as if they were to be gassed at the stroke of twelve.

I sipped my champagne. After a while Vito turned to watch the screen. I pushed the saucer of champagne closer to him. He did not respond. We both watched in silence.

There was an abrupt cutaway from the dance floor to a semi-hysterical anchor man standing on top of a mobile truck at the north end of Times Square. "We've switched away from the Taft Hotel and here we are in Times Square, thronged, even with the heavy snow, absolutely jam-packed with curb-to-curb people. And in less than one minute"—as he continued the cameras swept over Times Square, which was, just as he'd declared, "absolutely jam-packed with curb-to-curb people."

The sound stepped up several decibels. The roar of the crowd increased, pierced now and then by individual horns, whistles, ratchets and other noisemakers, then suddenly burst into a mass blast of a scream as the cameras zoomed in to the top of the Allied Chemical Building. "And there goes the ball of light and the count-down begins: ten, nine, eight, seven . . ."

The skin prickled up my back and down my arms because I'm a sucker and because we've been emotionally trained to regard this as a moment of great import.

"Four, three, two AND *ONE*—HAPPY NEW YEAR!"

As all hell broke loose in Times Square, I picked up my horn and aimed it at Vito's ear. He was aware of my move but did not budge. To my surprise I found I hadn't the heart to blow it. The cameras cut back and forth to catch individual scenes: a sailor with a bottle in each hand, his outstretched arms encircling three girls, a father hoisting a small boy up on his shoulders, an elderly couple locked in embrace.

I glanced outside the window at the snow falling so quietly. The hysteria on television was so far removed from us, there in my loft. It did not seem to be taking place on the same planet. We could have been looking down on it from a space station.

Vito suddenly turned his head to the side, facing away from the set and me.

The picture cut back to the dance floor where the couples now dragged their way through "Auld Lang Syne." Vito's shoulders appeared to be moving slightly. When "Auld Lang Syne" ended to generous applause, the band struck up a polka. Vito's shoulders now shook noticeably. I could hear no sound coming from him, but to make sure I leaned forward and switched off the set.

A cry from Vito, part anger, part something else: "Keep it on!"

I switched the set back on. He did his best to control himself, gagging and choking back what wanted out. But soon the game was up and he lay there sobbing convulsively.

I watched him closely, taking the whole sight of him in. There was something, the combination of his socks, his bare legs and behind, his wrists tied behind him, and then the pointed purple and silver hat on top of his head, that was the very essence of, to be perfectly honest—hurt little boy.

For the few moments I allowed myself to look, the sight of him, turned away from me, was incredibly moving. There was an impulse to reach over and touch him. Children crying, that's expected; a woman's tears are bad enough; but the sound of a man's sobs travels directly from my ear to my stomach.

I hated myself for this reaction, named it "sucker." Shook it off. He had no right to make me feel—*I had no right* to react in such a disgustingly maudlin way.

I stopped looking at him, picked up my champagne, sipped it, then put it down. I had no taste for it. I switched to a more tolerable emotion—annoyance—and turned the television off.

"Jesus, have a heart!"

I stood up. "For Christ's sake, what's the matter!"

"What's the *matter*?" After a short fit of coughing, he cleared his throat. "What's the *matter*? Nothin', nothin', I got a *hangnail*! What's the matter?" He kept his head turned away from me. He coughed again, gagged a bit, then spoke: "Shit, can't even blow my own—"

"Wait." I quickly tore off some paper toweling, went to him and held it up while he blew his nose.

"Thanks."

I got fresh toweling and wiped off his damp face; I also took off his paper hat.

He sucked in a deep breath and exhaled it shakily. "What's the matter! I *planned* on spending New Year's Eve like this. Didn't you know? Christ, I made my reservations in fucking *October*! Just to be sure I wouldn't miss it." He sniffed, clearing his nose. "What's the matter! My whole fucking life's the matter!"

I picked up my glass and tilted it up to his mouth. "Here . . ."

He sipped from it, swallowed, sipped again. "Thanks," he said, "you're a real *prince*." I smiled and offered him another drink, which he took. When he finished, he said, "I was even lookin' forward to tonight. I even had a booking."

"A *booking*?"

"Yeah, a *booking*!" he repeated, with a touch of defiance, despite his red eyes and blotchy face.

"What kind of a booking?"

"Little thing I do." A slight shrug of his shoulders. "Like a little show."

"A show?" I asked, not without surprise.

"Yeah—what?—you think you're the only actor? I do shows, a show now and then. I get fifty, seventy-five bucks. Tonight I was gettin' seventy-five, and once I even got *three hundred*." He tended to dispense amazing facts with the challenging chin-jutting bravado of a child: *You went to the movies Saturday? I went to* TWO *movies Saturday and* ONE *Sunday!*

He thought for a moment. "Tonight—tonight I'd have knocked down seventy-five, plus probably a twenty-five tip."

"What do you do?"

"Oh, a little routine—with a few jokes, one-liners."

"What kind of routine?"

"Oh, just—nothin' special." My questioning look brought forth a bark of laughter. "That's a hot one. Here I am, tied-down, bare-assed, and I'm pussyfootin' the issue." He laughed again. "Shit—who cares? Like a strip, kind of—but I don't take it all off. Oh, no, nothin' like that. 'Cept once when I was really bombed. Just down to the shorts, that's why the fancy ones. I got a breakaway leather outfit, it's stashed uptown. So I had this gig up on the West Side, a bunch of fruits and some assorted dykes."

I could not believe my ears.

He went on, more mulling the figures over to himself. "Yeah, seventy-five I'd have made, plus probably another twenty-five tip. Yeah, I'd have come out of it with Big Bill, a hundred."

"Why didn't you tell me?" (I don't know where that came from.)

"Hah, you'd have let me go, huh? In a pig's ass. Yeah, an' I believe in sex after death, too!"

I faced him. "If you stood to make a hundred dollars, what were you doing robbing me again?"

"Listen, I said I did a show *now and then*. I didn't say I was any big Broadway star. I work parties, I get 'em by reference, maybe one or two a month. Maybe not. Big deal. BFD."

I still could not get over this latest bit of information. "Doing a *strip tease*?"

"Listen, it's no minty strip. I mean it's done with humor, but I play it tough. Men dig it. Yeah, it gets 'em hot. Women, too. Why shouldn't women see a guy strip? Let 'em have their lib. Gals are always taking it off for the guys, why shouldn't a guy show a little skin for them? Women like it."

What sort of creature did I have tied up here? My spirits were light and heady again. The pill was working. I felt high, the kind of high you get from finding a ten-dollar bill on the floor of a cab. I looked at him for a long time. "What's the story with you anyhow?"

He blinked his eyes; the fun disappeared entirely. "Hmnn . . . you want to know the story? Last week I walked into this paper store on the corner near where I used to live. I was all spaced out, comin' down from a bad trip. The old lady runs the place, white hair, granny glasses, false teeth that kill her, the whole bit, got to be seventy, seventy-five, looks like George Washington in drag, sweet old thing. She takes me in from across the candy counter, looks at me for a good long zap, then says, 'Well, that's the way it goes, huh, baby—shit and more shit!' " He flicked his eyes up at me, using them as exclamation points.

"And . . . ?"

"That's it, that's what she wrote, beginning, middle and end."

"That bad, huh? If you could have one wish on New Year's—I mean outside of getting untied—what would it be?"

"You mean right now?"

"Yes."

He looked me directly in the eye and without hesitation said: "Makin' it with you."

Amazed, I could only ask, "What?"

He spit out, the toughness of his speech completely contradicting the meaning of his words: "You *heard* me—*makin' it with you!*"

"You're kidding! Why?"

"Why not? You're here, an' I sure in the fuck am! That's for openers. But mainly 'cause when I'm depressed, makin' it takes my mind off *why* I'm depressed. You want more reasons, I'll give 'em to you." He ducked his head back as much as he could; it was a gesture of appraisal. "You're humpy in a offbeat sort of way."

I laughed. "*I'm* offbeat? *You're* calling *me* offbeat?"

"Yeah, you're—you got this—something very—ah—vulnerable. That's the word. Something nice and vulnerable, like they just took the bandages off."

This was too much, this was upside down and backward. After

the way I'd felt about him only seconds before, now he was labeling *me*—vulnerable! "Jesus, if you don't take the—"

"I ain't finished yet," he said. "Also, I overheard your references for—ah, Hugglebunnyburgers. Oh, that's a pisser!" He hooted a bit over that. "I turn out good ones, too, so between us, I figure we'd ring the bell, have a hit on our hands." He jerked his head in the direction of the bed. "So, come on, whyn't you let me up and we'll, you know, toss the old salad."

I looked at him and shook my head. "I can't get over you being—well, queer."

No annoyance in his reply. He merely sloughed it off. "Queer—shit! Queer, not queer. Who's countin'? Who cares, that's old-fashioned, that went out with saddle shoes. Oh, that's right, I forget, you're thirty-eight, you belong to that in-between generation, the lost one, yeah, you come in right at the ass end of it, didn't you? Queer, I told you, everybody swings, the right moment, the right place, the right circumstances. Christ, don't give me that 'Oh-my-shocked-ass-you're-queer' shit. Are *you* queer?"

"No."

"Hmn . . . too bad, you don't know what you're missing." Then: "You *never* fooled around, I mean with a guy? Truth now—or your dick will fall off."

I was still too stunned to make sense. "Well . . ." I began.

Vito laughed, making up the dialogue for me. "Well, yeah, in high school, there was this one guy, but we was only kids and all we did was whack off." He laughed again. "Then once when I was drunk this guy blew me, but I was so bombed I didn't even know what was happening. Hmn . . . hmn . . . I know the rest, I heard it before. Blah-blah-blah-blah-blah-blah-blah-blah"—he punctuated the series with a Bronx cheer—"youse guys kill me."

"And youse kill me," I told him.

"Why do you make fun of me?" he asked, seriously.

"Why do you say 'youse'?"

"I know, I know better. I don't know why. Main reason—habit

which I never got out of." I could tell by the wise look spreading over his face that he was returning to topic A. "Hmn . . . you ever been married?"

"No."

"And thirty-eight! Hmn? Well, I have. Married at seventeen, got a daughter nine, so don't give me that queer bit. Save that for people ain't been around the block twice."

"A daughter nine?"

"Yeah, Melody Antenucci." He shook his head. "Ain't that a pisser to hang on a kid? Not my idea, my wife's. Queer! My friend Ben said queer is a word like tall. Everybody's a little tall, even midgets, it's *how* tall. He used to say if you could peek at any man or woman in their privacy of their bathroom alone, gettin' ready to go to bed or gettin' up in the morning—he used to say, *then* you'd see some queer little things goin' on. Little private weirdo iggies would banjo your eyes."

"Who's this Ben?"

"My lover, he bought the farm. He's with the Kennedy boys now." (From the way he tossed off the last, I got the idea he was displaying his worldliness.)" Only good thing ever happened and then—" He was quiet for a moment; suddenly in a burst of energy he said: "*He* was a writer, Benjamin Bergmann?"

If anything he'd said astonished me, this was the capper. "Benjamin—he was your *lover*?"

His back was up. "Yeah, what's so funny about that? Oh, because he was married to that French actress? He was married twice, had three kids—how could he be queer, huh? Jesus, you really are from the old country, aren't you?" He was quiet once more; I said nothing because I hadn't the slightest idea what to make of him. "But Ben—he really had a peek at the blueprints. He seen the elephant and heard the hooty owl." He looked up at me. "And—you know what else?"

"What?"

"He really dug me." He nodded his head in assent with his own declaration. "Jesus, he was something else. He—talk about vivid."

The phone rang.

"Probably that cunty aunt of yours." His hoarse bark. "Fuckin' point killer!"

The sound of her voice made me grin. "Hello, Claire." I glanced at Vito, who crossed his eyes. Claire, still suspicious of my absence, could hear the smile in my voice and lost no time asking if Kate was there. I reiterated that we had broken up. Was I alone? Yes. Was I really *all alone on New Year's Eve*? Yes.

There was a good bit of clucking over this, how it wasn't New Year's Eve without "my only real family." She was leaving the next afternoon for a two-week vacation in Tobago; she extended an invitation, which I declined.

"Jimmy, with the play falling through, it would do you good to get away."

It would do me good to get away, but not with Claire. "I'd like to, Claire, but I just can't."

"Why not, dear?"

"I've lost my job, I have to start looking for a place to live, and I—"

"Just for two weeks, then we'll come back and get everything straightened out. I'll go apartment-hunting with you."

"I can't, Claire. I have to stay here and figure out what to do."

"About another apartment? Well, that's not so—"

"No, about my *life!*"

"Now, Jimmy, I know you've had some disappointments, but you know you can always count on me. Matter of fact I had a little check, just a little New Year's present, all ready for you. I'll put it in the mail—"

"No, please don't, Claire, I'm all right."

"Just a little New Year's present from me to you."

I wished her a good vacation in Tobago and said I'd see her when she got back in two weeks.

I was muddled by the ambiguity of my feelings. I didn't want to accept money from her, still I knew she would put the check in the mail, and I couldn't help wondering how much it would be for. I felt, if not outright dirty, at least a bit—dusty.

"What's Tobago?" Vito asked.

"An island."

"Never heard of it. So—you don't want to go, I'll go. She like to get shtupped? I'll even shtupp her."

"Mmn, I could see the two of you together. As for the—what, shtupping?—I think it's closed for the season."

"Yeah, you never can tell. Don't ever try to put a lid on an old volcano. Just when you do, she'll blow! Hey, could you ease me up here? This ain't exactly the position of your dreams, you know."

I walked over to him. "Where's it uncomfortable?"

"You kiddin'? All over."

The telephone rang again.

"Way she keeps callin', I think she wants to get into your knickers."

It was not Claire; it was Kate. "Happy New Year," she said.

"Happy New Year." I could hear party sounds in the background.

"So, how's everything going?"

"Fine," I said. "And with you?"

"Fine."

We had put in too much time together to play it straight; there was a long silence before we both burst into laughter.

"Oh, Jim—really—you're—I mean—that was—*Fred* was—*what was all that?*" This said on the waves of her laughter, thus keeping it light and mirthful, hoping to make it almost a *mutual* joke. And thereby sneak the answer out of me.

But I knew her so well, knew that underneath the laughter her gears were absolutely jammed.

"Kate, I—really can't go into it now. It's, well—" although I still laughed, I pulled my voice down to a whisper—"there are a couple of other people here now and I—"

"Other?" she asked. No laughter now.

"Yes, and ah—I can't—look, we'll talk."

I hung up.

"Ohh," Vito said, "you're a pisser, oh, you are a pisser, Jimmy Zoole!" Then: "What a name for an actor—Zoole!"

The phone rang again. I picked it up. Now her voice was sharp and clear. *"Jim, now you listen to me—"*

I whispered into the phone. "Kate, I can't talk now . . ." I broke the connection and left the receiver off the hook.

"Oh, God," I told Vito, "curiosity has been nibbling away at her. Nibbling—it's been gnawing at her." Her call had boosted me up to the next level.

"Serves her right," Vito said. "Hey, you said you'd ease me up here."

"I'm not going to let you up, though."

"Who asked you? I got no place to go," he said, as I set about loosening the backstraps slightly. "I already missed my booking. I don't even have a steady mattress now."

"Where have you been sleeping?"

"Anyplace, around."

"But you had twenty-seven dollars in your pocket."

"I just got it, guy—about a half hour before I dropped in on you."

"How?" I asked.

"Snatched a purse."

"You mean, just from a woman walking down the—"

He snapped his head around to me. "No, a *dog*, a little French poodle was trottin' down Christopher Street with this *purse* and I—"

"Ah-ah, no lip!" I warned. I'd loosened the backstraps so he could move slightly to the left or right and at least flex his back and raise his shoulders.

"That's better, thanks."

I stepped away from him. "So you snatched a purse from a helpless woman?"

"Sure a woman. Okay, yeah, I know what you're thinking. But let me tell you something, I don't go in for purse-snatching. This was special, New Year's Eve, and I'll tell you something else. I never snatched a purse yet from anyone didn't look like they could afford it."

"What does that mean?"

"It means what it says. I pick someone that I know their cookie jar is full. Like this one, sure she was tiny *and* she was old, but she had on a good fur coat, mink, weighed more than she did, one of those that dip down in back and skin the ground. And that wild blue hair that she didn't whip up over any kitchen sink *and* expensive suede bad-feet shoes. Twenty-seventy bucks wouldn't mean dick to her." I only looked at him. "Honest, Jimmy."

He was seriously trying to convince me that he had ethics of a sort. "Still," I said, "a little old woman."

"Listen, I bet it made her whole New Year's. She probably didn't have diddily-squat to do, now she's got something to quack about, probably the biggest New Year's she'd had in about a century. She got an interview with the cops, they probably gave her coffee, the works. Feisty, too. I had to give it to her. Yelled out 'Stop thief!'—the whole bit. Christ, she was bow-legged, you could ride a bike between 'em. I looked back just as I turned the corner and she was rackin' at me at a fast waddle." He giggled. "Looked like she was on a teeter-totter."

Although I didn't approve, I found myself getting a kick out of his account. I realized I was having—if not the best of times—most certainly an unusual one.

"Hey," Vito said, "couldn't you untie just my hands? You still got my feet tied and my legs and back—my shoulders are broke, this position is a bitch!"

"No funny stuff?"

"Truth." (Troot.) As I loosened the knot that held his wrists together behind his back, he said: "Hey, then let's have a smoke, get a little high—huh?"

I believe it was Kate's phone call that allowed me to say, "Why not?"

He swung his head around, his face lighted up. "You mean it?"

"Sure."

"Nifty! Hey, I can't wait to see you high. Some people just holler out to get high. I bet you make a great head."

"I don't think it works with me."

"Bat shit! But I warn you, if you get high, you'll let me up."

"I'll bet I don't."

"Betcha. If I win, you got to make it with me."

"And if I win?" I asked.

"*I* gotta make it with *you!*"

"You're a card, all right." The knot was untied; I released his hands. "There."

"Whew!" He drew his arms from around his back to the sides, then to the front, flexing his fingers. "Ohh, boy. Hey, you really gonna smoke?"

"Sure, I said I would, didn't I?"

A slight moment of trepidation over two items. I knew if I smoked I would lose at least part of my control. After all, that was the whole *point* of smoking. The other, there was an enormous difference now that his hands were untied and he was able to use his arms. He stretched his arms way out from his sides, then flexed his fingers again. There was great freedom in the gesture. I wasn't sure whether I wanted him to be *that* free.

Jesus, that hurts, feels like my shoulders was busted." He looked at me and spoke in retroactive anger. "Goddamn it, why'd you have to tie 'em back like that? I'm all stiff. How'd you like to be tied down with *your* hands behind *you*?"

"Wait a minute, I untie you and now I have to take a lot of lip."

He smiled. "Yeah, I didn't say thanks, did I?" He laughed, stretching his arms out in front of him and flexing his fingers again. "Great, I can play the violin again. Ahh—!" He cracked his knuckles. "Ohh, I've been dying to do that. It was drivin' me buggy not to be able to crack 'em."

"Why didn't you tell me, I'd have cracked them for you."

"Yeah, I bet." He crossed his eyes, gave his knuckles a good resounding crack, and said, "Okay, gimme that little plastic bag with the goodies."

I brought him the bag, which he opened, then sniffed. "Wait'll you get a load of Senegalese Thunderfuck! Hey, you never been high, for real? Come on, truth!" I shook my head. "Jesus, you're *retarded*!" He began rolling the joints.

His attitude niggled me slightly, but I let it pass. "Tell me about your wife."

"Ex, she's remarried. Marcy. Oh, God, did I love her. You heard about Romeo and Juliet, well, that was us. In a scroungy East Harlem sorta way. We met on a fire escape on East 112th Street. I was sixteen, she was fifteen. Bammo, it was love! If I didn't see her for a day I wouldn't eat. I thought she hung the moon.

"And *she* loved *me*. Tender, talk about tender. I felt so tender about her I'd just bust out crying. First time we did it, on top of the roof where she lived, one hot summer night under about a quadrillion stars—she was a virgin, so it took a long time to—you know, because I didn't want to hurt her and I ain't exactly built like a midget—but when I did, you know, work it in, I just—all I could do was *cry*. I just lay there on top of her and cried, then all during the main bout I was crying and even for the finale I cried. I just loved her so much.

"After that we made"—he broke off, laughing on the straight line of a high Hee—"Hugglebunnyburgers! Hey, were you kiddin' with that? That's a corker!"

"I hope so," I told him.

"Yeah, you gotta. Anyway we made Hugglebunnyburgers—like they was going out of style. On the roof, in the basement, on the fire escape, down by the East River, over by the Department of Sanitation, the balcony Loew's Eighty-sixth Street—and you know where else? In the tulip beds right in the middle of Park Avenue!"

"Right in that center place?"

He finished rolling one joint, held it up for inspection, and began on another. "Yeah, we went there to swipe some flowers for her mother's birthday and we seen a cop car cruising along so we ducked down in 'em and—one thing led to another. What a wild scene, traffic whizzing by, those huge buildings all lighted up sticking up on both sides and us in a clinch, snuggled down in the goddam tulips!"

He shrugged off the happy memory of that episode; the corners of his mouth turned down. "But, you see, when she got pregnant with Melody—after her old man and brother beat the holy crap outta me"—he opened his mouth and thumped the upper left teeth with his index finger—"those three teeth here. A bridge. The Frank and Timothy Ryan Memorial Bridge, I call it. When I got over that, my old man hadda get into the act. He beat me up, almost as bad." Vito shrugged, passed it off with: "Saturday night, nothin' *else* to do. Followin' Friday *her* old man beat up *my* old man, that Sunday afternoon *my* brother, Sal, beat up *her* brother, Tim.

"So, bein' everyone loved everyone else—we got married! Catholics, the old-country Wop and Mick kind, Christ, if a gorilla banged their daughter and they could *catch* him—zap, get 'em to the church on time. 'But, Daddy, I don't want to marry no gorilla!' 'Shut up and put on your veil, you fucked a gorilla, you're gonna marry a gorilla!'

"So—we got married, set up in a little cold-water flat of our own, Cockroach Heaven, East 109th Street. Me, happy as a piss clam at high tide, workin' as a busboy in a deli afternoons and nights, other odd jobs during the day. The baby comes and right like that, the Big Freeze. Marcy's blood turns to ice water. She and the baby in the bedroom, I'm out on a daybed in the living room. Suddenly she's goin' to church every five minutes and not only that, suddenly she's got lockjaw of the legs. Makes me beg for it. Now she'd only let me sleep with her—like, as a reward. If I painted the kitchen or signed up for night school. And when she did let me, she'd lay there like she was puttin' on a brave show for the dentist."

Vito held the second joint up for inspection "One more and we're all set. The baby, Melody, got all the affection. I could understand, in a way, but understandin' up in the attic"—Vito tapped his forehead—"don't help clear the rocks outta the heart. Listen, sixteen and seventeen, that's what we were by then, married's a bummer anyhow you look at it. I tell you, Jimmy—"

Again I experienced a strange sensation hearing my name spoken with such familiarity.

"Truth now. The reason I first started pulling little heists was to get extra bread so's I could come up with presents for her and the baby, so maybe she'd let me spend the night in my own bed, for Chrissake. Finally, one night she done something very mean in a personal way. My birthday and she was letting me sleep with her. Jesus, when I think how I kept on beggin'! Anyhow, while we was makin' it, *I* was makin' it, it was strictly a one-man operation, she suddenly slips a magazine out from under her pillow—I never forget, it had Elvis Presley on the cover—and starts leafin' through it. You *believe*! I'm makin' love to Elvis Presley—" He barked his sore-throat laugh. "Elvis Presley! And I wasn't even swingin' at the time! I slapped her, first time I ever laid a hand—truth, Jimmy. Another first that night, first time I ever felt I could hate her. A good feelin', least that way I could empty the rocks outta my heart. Christ, I had a whole gravel pit workin' for me. A few months more and I split, I hadda."

"What about Melody, you miss her?"

"Dumb question number one. What a little—like a little porce-lain doll she is. She—" He broke off abruptly. "Okay, we had the eulogy, don't wanna get heavy. Okay?" He held up the third ciga-rette. "Come on, light up for New Year's. First one gets high wins Jane Fonda's jockey shorts!"

Vito handed me the cigarette. As I struck a match and lighted up, he said, "Now take in air with it, suck it down, way down, and hold it down!"

"I know how to do it, it just doesn't work." I took a deep drag. The second the smoke touched bottom I coughed it up—violently. I could hardly have made a worse showing.

He held out his hand. "Here, watch. Christ, you smoke like that little old bowlegged lady on Christopher Street."

"But you, you know how to smoke pot, snatch purses, rob apartments, screw and get screwed probably, but give you ten thousand in a checking account and you wouldn't even know how to get it out—dumb-ass! What are some of your other worldly accomplishments, what else do you know how to do, O Wise One?"

Vito looked at me for a count of five before speaking in a quiet, flat voice. "Get even with you. Show you mean for mean. Sometime—you'll see."

I awarded him points. "Touché, I didn't mean to get—heavy." My outburst had surprised me.

Back to his conversational tone: "That's the purpose of the smoking lesson. We're gonna get light, light, light—up and over. O-Wise-One will now continue with the course. Pot Smoking One. In spite of the snotty pupil." He took a deep drag, held it down, and spoke in a strangulated ventriloquist's voice without expelling a trace of smoke: "You take it way in, suck it down, and hold it down with all you got, the stomach muscles, hold it, hold it, just like you was holdin' back a fart in an elevator."

"You're a regular poet," I told him.

"Yeah," he said, expelling a small mushroom cloud of smoke and handing me the cigarette. "I told Ben I was gonna pen my memoirs. Call it *Tough Shit! The Story of My Life So Far.*" He sounded a semi-moronic teenager's laugh. "There, go ahead. Make Daddy proud of you."

I inhaled deeply, held it down with all my might. It stayed several seconds before tickling my stomach into releasing it.

"Look, you gotta—"

"Shut up!" I snapped. "The first time you performed *fellatio* did you do it well? Or do you even know what that means?"

"Yes, I do. And, yes, I did. Want to see how—come here!"

I shook my head at him, took another drag, held it down, down, down. It wanted to come up but I contracted my stomach, forcing the muscles in and down. When I felt I could no longer hold without coughing, I exhaled slowly.

"Good," Vito said. "You're gonna get a gold star and if you're *extra* good, you're gonna get to stay after school and do naughties with the teacher."

My laughter expelled the smoke. "Jesus, you have a one-track mind." I coughed up the rest. "You're a great help."

"Yeah, Ben said if I could channel my sex drive to something else—like real estate, I'd be another Levittown or whatever his name was." He took the joint from me and inhaled deeply. I envied the way he could talk and hold the smoke down inside at the same time. "An' I just might, one of these days, if I can ever stop scramblin'."

"Scrambling?"

"Yeah, scramblin' for food, for a pad, scramblin' to get high, for a warm body, for some new threads. Scramblin' for someone to hook up with mainly. I always like to be hooked up with someone. If I could ever quit scramblin' for about ten minutes then I'd have time to figure out what to do with my fucked-up self." He finally expelled the smoke and handed me the cigarette.

"You get high a lot?" I asked.

"Often as I can."

"Why?" I took another deep drag; my stomach was warmed up; it accepted the smoke now without kicking back.

"For the main reason"—I don't know why I got such a kick out of that phrase but I did—"I like it. Another main issue—I forget. I forget my old lady and my old man, pissers the both of them. I get high to forget how stupid I been, to forget Marcy and Melody— oow, what a name to hang on a kid! To forget a lot of things I done, to forget Ben. Uh-uh, but him I can't forget."

"Oww—ohh!" A wave of dizziness rippled across my forehead, then wrapped itself around my head. I grabbed hold of the sink unit to steady myself. "Whew—hey!" I blinked my eyes and focused. Vito was laughing. I felt as if I'd been standing on my head and had been swung abruptly to my feet; only my stomach had not quite caught up with the move. I had an impulse to laugh, also, but

I didn't. This was an all-time first. I was getting high. But with whom, friend or foe?

Another wave hit. I held on to the sink. Vito was still laughing. I looked into his eyes, but I couldn't read them. Was he laughing with, at, or because of me, or because of what would happen? And while I was there, what *would* happen when I was thoroughly stoned?

A scary moment of uncertainty grabbed me. I was entering unknown territory—no, I was *in* it, I'd already stuck one foot in, a wobbly foot. If I could have taken it back out, I would have. But there was no taking it back, the stuff was already in my system.

I was standing very close to him, so close I could feel his body warmth, or else I imagined I could. It seemed like a good idea to move away. I let go of the sink and sidled over to the small kitchen table and held on to it.

I just got a—like a tremor. Oh, yes, I feel it. But—so soon?"

Vito was delighted. "Sure, so soon. Didn't I tell you? Senegalese Thunderfuck don't stall around, it gets the goodies straight to the customer, no middle man. You okay?"

"Yes, I think." I felt warm inside and a good twenty pounds lighter.

"Here, take another puff to cinch it." I did, took a deep one, held it down, until the warm feeling increased to a mild burn. Then I exhaled. "Yeah, you done good." Vito dragged deep, again speaking with the smoke inside him. "Don't need much—three, four good drags and you're on your way."

"Ummm," was all I felt like saying. "Ummm . . ."

Vito exhaled and laughed. "Here, let me see your eyes." I faced him. "Naw, come here, up close, I ain't gonna bite you!" I stepped over to him and leaned down. He cackled. "Hee . . . you're on your way! Yeah, your eyes look like Crazy Cat."

I had a feeling I must look like the reflection from a funhouse mirror. The ripples must be showing. I glanced at Vito; not a ripple in sight. "Don't you feel it?" I asked.

"Sure, but I'm used to it."

"But you look the same."

"So do you, 'cept for your eyes!"

"I do? I don't *feel* the same."

"You better *not*, this stuff is expensive."

I felt a medium-sized quake. "Whew—I know what I have to do!" It was urgent that I sit. "I have to sit down." I flopped into the armchair I'd dragged over in front of the TV set. Feeling a larger quake, I grabbed hold of the arms.

"That's only the first big blast, the rocket stage. Then you go into a nice easy orbit. It evens off."

"I hope." I quickly stood up. "There was—*something*—I was going to do something."

Vito laughed. "You was gonna sit down!"

I slapped my forehead. "That's right. Oh—*oh, I already was sitting!* Oh, Jesus, I'm losing my mind. Maybe—maybe you should have started me off on something not so, you know, a little lessel—" I giggled and sat down again. "A *little lesser*—"

"Don't sweat it, you'll be fine."

"Oh, I feel fine." And I did. Never finer. "Oh, do I feel fine! Fine as a Fiddler's Fuck." The phrase titillated me. "Is that an expression—'Fine as a Fiddler's Fuck'?"

"Search me, it is now."

"Fine as a Fiddler's Fuck. Yeah, I think it is. But then—why would a Fiddler's Fuck be any finer than, say, a Plumber's Fuck or a Truck Driver's? Fine as a *Plumber's Fuck*? No, it's flat, doesn't have that certain—zip. Fine as a *Fiddler's Fuck* is—perky!" I was off and running. "Okay, the curtain goes up on the first scene and the Grande Dame of the manor is serving tea in the sun room to Pastor Goodheart. Bam, in through the French door bounces the comely daughter of the house. Ah—Melody? Yes, Melody!"

"Uck!" from Vito.

"In a smashing tennis outfit, all out of breath. And the Mater says, 'Ah, Melody, what a surprise! How are you, darling?' 'Fine as a Fiddler's Fuck, Mother dear, and you?' 'Ditto, Angel-Bumps, you know Pastor Goodheart'—and so forth, blah-blah-blah-blah-blah-blah-blah-blah-blah-blah!" I ended with the Bronx cheer, courtesy of Vito, who got a proper kick out of it.

"But," I went on, "if Melody had said, 'Fine as a *Plumber's* Fuck'—it would louse up the whole scene, stop it cold. The Lady of the Manor would have to say, *'Darling, not in front of Pastor Goodheart!'* It would change the entire opening of the play, make it too heavy, too—blech! 'Fine as a *Plumber's* Fuck!' " I turned to Vito. "All wrong, don't you think?"

"Oh, boy, are you gonna be a great head!"

"Yeah, how can you tell?"

"How can I tell! Three, four puffs and you're off and runnin'—all by your own. I didn't have to do diddily-squat."

"Well, *someone* has to keep the ball going." Suddenly Vito looked ridiculous lying there, chin in his pillow, ass to the ceiling. "Don't just lie there—say something! Oh . . ." I stood up and stretched out my arms. "I feel like I could fly!"

"If flying's your point, go to it. Take off."

"No, wait . . ." I held my arms straight out and lifted up on my toes. "Levitate, it's more a feeling that if I breathed *just right*—I could levitate." Suddenly I was lost. "What were we talking about?"

Vito grinned. "Fine as a Fiddler's Fuck."

"Oh, yeah. Fine as a Fiddler's Fuck. Sure." I was relieved to remember. I was just as quickly unsettled when the sentence, familiar though it seemed, remained hanging in limbo, without connection to past, present, or future. "How did we get onto that?"

"Search me."

"Vito, I feel like a silly ass."

"So, groove on it. Better than feelin' like a dead-ass."

"Yes, I know, but I'm *acting* like a silly ass." I could not help giggling. "I know it, but I can't help it. Okay, I'm gonna settle down." It now seemed imperative to latch on to a nonfrivolous subject. "Ah—Ben! *Yes*, tell me about Ben."

"Ben, okay—"

"Fine as a Fiddler's Fuck, huh? Why is 'fuck' such an unattractive word for such a nifty pastime?"

"I don't know," Vito said, "but whoever invented it sure knew what they were doing. Ben said the two best inventions in the world was fucking and peppermint-stick ice cream."

In the light of sanity that combination is not all that devastating, but to me, right then, it was hysterically funny.

There is usually felt a connection between mind and body; this connection had been broken now and my mind was floating free and clear, soaring balloonlike. If there was a link to my body, it was only the slightest silken thread that held us together. It was a lovely sensation, with only one minor drawback: I kept losing my point, if point I had. When I stopped laughing, I was lost again. "What were we talking about? I thought I had a point. Or *you* had a point. Somebody had one, didn't they?" Before he could answer I stood up. "Jesus, I wish Pete was here."

"Pete?" Vito asked.

"Yes, a friend of mine." I looked at Vito, felt a sudden rush of wanting to tell him everything: Pete, my mother, Claire, Kate, my career even. Dump it all out, the way a drunk sitting at a bar spills the works to a stranger, little news flashes he would never drop on his wife or even his best friend.

As I stood there thinking this over, Vito spoke: "Go ahead, say it."

"Say what?" I quickly asked, wondering if he'd read my mind.

"Whatever you were gonna say, you were off on some kind of trip by yourself. That ain't fair, say it."

I wouldn't tell him everything, but I would—talk. "Well, okay—" But my point kept changing: now this came out: "I have a feeling of—wanting to confront my enemies. No, of wanting to confront the *enemy part* of my friends."

"Like how?"

"Like, saying to Claire, 'Look, Claire, keep your money, don't keep promising to leave it to me. Take it *with* you. I still dig the good part of you—but don't bombard me with the Jews, the Blacks, the Rotten Young People, how the country and everything else is going to hell. Keep the gloomy stuff to yourself, I can't listen any more.'

"Then—well, Kate. 'Look, old girl, thanks for the good times, of which there were many, but you really ought to cool the mouth on you, swallow an opinion now and then, simmer down. Or you'll never find a husband who'll put up with you. Oh, yes, and—once you told me I ought to come on in the real world more like I do when I'm screwing, stronger, more sure of myself. Well, you—you ought to act more like *you* do when *you're* screwing. Warmer, more giving, softer.'" I turned to Vito. "Damnit, why didn't I ever tell her *that*!"

He only grinned; he was getting a kick out of my ramblings; I didn't mind in the least. The performer in me liked it, which led to:

"Then I'd like to do a musical audition right now. *Right now!* They usually scare hell out of me. I shake so much—Vito, I could strap cymbals to the insides of my knees and accompany myself. But now, right now, I'd like to plant my two feet center stage and belt out a few." I laughed. "I would."

"Go ahead, be my guest."

But the focus kept shifting. "No, the hell with acting! See, what I'd like to do is get away, away *someplace*, just hole up and write my book. Write it and have it there for all time. Performances, they evaporate, you can't find 'em, but a book, there it is, you can hold it. It sticks around."

I turned to face Vito squarely. "Jesus, you bastard!" He flinched. I laughed. "You took the book, threw it away, and didn't even have the decency to *read* it! Threw it away and I don't even get a god-damn *opinion*!" I laughed louder and cupped my hands, raising them to my mouth and imitating a bullhorn. "Now, hear this, will the bastard who swiped my novel please have the guts to read it!"

When I calmed down, Vito said, in a low voice: "Hey, come here..."

"I was just kidding."

"That don't matter, come here."

I walked over and stood in front of him. "Lord God Almighty, if it makes you feel this good, they really ought to legalize it. I'm gonna address the joint houses of Congress! Hey, I made a pun—*joint* houses, get it?"

No smile from Vito. "Yeah, well"—he reached out and took one of my hands, clasping it firmly with both of his—"I want to tell youse something—"

I laughed; he squeezed my hand harder. "No, for serious. See, what with Ben and all, I know something about writers and writin'. What it means. Truth, Jimmy, if I'd have known what those pages was I never would have heaved them out, never. I was so strung out when I ripped you off that time, I didn't even know what I was doin'. I don't even remember throwing the pages out or where. All I remember was, I needed money to buy stuff, anything I could hock or—I never would have, in my right mind." His and Kate's green eyes looked up at me. "You believe me?"

"Yes."

"Honest, especially now that I met you." He looked down at my hand. "I really dig you, guy." He lowered his head, pressing his cheek against my hand.

The combination, rather contradiction, of the warmth of his cheek (and this gesture) and the strength in his hands as he held mine unnerved me. I tried to pull away. He quickly lifted his head, at the same time increasing his grip on my hand. When he saw the look on my face, he was immediately annoyed. "Hey, not so fast," he snapped, back to his old toughness. He grabbed me by the wrist. Then *he* laughed. "Hah, Jesus, that's a good one, here I am tied down and *I got you scared.* Haven't I? What are you scared of—me saying I dig you, or touching you?"

"Yes."

"Which—or both?" He tightened his grip.

"Yes."

"Or maybe how you might feel if I really tried something . . . ?" He squeezed my wrist until it hurt. "Huh . . . ?"

Oddly enough it made me laugh as I said, "Yeah, maybe that, too."

He let go of me. "Touché yourself. Don't worry—or maybe you think I'm so far beneath you, this crum here ain't *fit* to touch you, or even say things. Is that it?"

"No, and you know it." I knew from the way his tone had turned so quickly defensive, he'd said that, or words equivalent, a hundred times before.

"So—what's the big deal? The touch of someone who digs you should—you should *dig* it."

While I was mulling that one over, he asked. "Quick, a penny— what are you thinking?"

I was thinking: We had a moment there.

Come on, a penny for what's up in the attic?"

"Nothing," I lied. "I was trying to think what we were talking about before . . . ah—"

"Before what?"

I laughed. "I don't even know *that*."

"Couple times you asked me to tell you about Ben, but then you kept on with the blah-blah-blah yourself."

"Yes, you were going to tell me about Ben." I remembered my interest in this, because I could not, in my wildest imaginings, picture Vito Antenucci and Benjamin Bergmann saying hello, let alone having—whatever they had.

"You want another joint first?"

"No, you'd have to scrape me off the ceiling. You have one, if you want."

"Hey, could you just loosen the strap around my back, just a little, so I could—you're breakin' my back!"

"Sure." As I stepped close to him I thought: not only that, I'm going to let you up. This whole Gulliver thing is ridiculous.

But I stopped in my tracks. If the major of smoking pot is a loosening, a freeing action, its minor is now and then a flash of paranoia. It occurred to me this was perhaps exactly what he was trying to get me to do, in his own underhanded way. In that case it became a point of honor to maintain control. "You're not trying to con me, are you?"

"No, guy, my back!"

"Don't try anything, we're getting along great, don't louse it up." I loosened the straps a bit, at least he could raise his shoulders slightly higher now. "If you try any tricks, I'll—"

"Yeah, what would you do?" Vito asked, cracking his knuckles.

"I don't know, sell you to the gypsies."

"Big deal, you'd have to pay *them*."

"You don't think much of yourself, do you?" I asked.

"What—you'd run me for president?"

"*Vice* president, maybe." That caused a wince. "Oh, that's not funny." I'd finished loosening the strap; I'd also checked to see that it was still secure. "There, that better?"

"Yeah, thanks." Vito adjusted his position. "See, that's what Ben was gonna do, teach me how to like myself. He said you really had to like yourself before you could clue in to the rest of the crowd. Main reason, you're always sold on old Number One the most, so if you don't like what's going on inside yourself, not much chance you're gonna dig what's goin' on with the whole gang. Right?"

"Right."

"See, I started hustlin' after I left Marcy. Didn't plan on it, just fell into it."

"How do you just fall into hustling?"

"Easy." He shrugged and gave his knuckles a few warm-up cracks. "I was delivering groceries for this pissy little market on Second Avenue in the Fifties. The kind where they do you a favor to sell you a tomato for a buck. Paid me next to nothin' but the tips was good. One day I drop off a carton of stuff to this townhouse on

Forty-ninth Street. I notice banjo eyes on the guy that lives there, then just as I'm goin' out the door, he drops the line: 'How'd you like to make fifty dollars?' Yes, I say, I don't even ask how. Christ, fifty bucks was as much as my week's salary. He tells me to drop back after work.

"Six o'clock, back I go. He showed me. Fifty bucks and I didn't even have to do nothin'; just lie there while this rich, good-looking *educated* guy took care of me. But what's more—was gettin' such a kick out of it! Now, Jimmy, I gotta tell you, *I* got a kick out of *that*, that *he* was gettin' such a kick. Ends up I walk out of there, plus the fifty, with some shirts, a bottle of vodka, plus he fed me dinner and *talked* to me, was really *interested* in me.

"Right away I figured I'd stumbled into my life's work. Truth! I really think that's right when I went the other way. I mean I didn't go exclusive that way, I always been double-gaited, but—you know, started makin' it with men. Especially after Marcy. Suddenly someone wants it so bad from me they *pay* me, they even load me down with affection. Wow, I got a bonus! I figure I'm onto a winner.

"So, I seen this guy several times, then he asked me to bartend at a big bash he threw and I met this other guy, Bobby, who really took the big fall for me. He and his partner were in wallpaper and pretty soon I signed on as their houseboy and after a while I even did the cooking. Hey, did youse know I'm a good cook?"

"No, was that on your résumé?"

"No shit, I am. I'm a gourmet cook. They sent me to the French Gourmet Cooking School. I already cooked good wop food."

A connection was made. "Cook, you *cook*?"

"Yeah, what's so funny?"

"Sure, did you take a little bundle of fresh dill *one* of the times you robbed me?"

His mouth dropped open. "Yeah, oh yeah, that's right, a nice little bunch of fresh dill all wrapped up in white paper." There was pride in his voice. "Yeah, that was me. Yeah, that's right. So I cooked for Bobby and Lyman, his partner, and bunked with Bobby. I hadda good deal, but—see, this is where dumb comes in! I got greedy. I never had any money and when I got a little, I went zonkers. Should of seen the clothes I bought. They paid me three hundred a month and I didn't have no expenses, three hundred clear off the top. But I never saved a penny. Also, get me out at a bar or a restaurant and Mr. Big had to pick up the check. Oh, yeah, Legs Diamond is back in town. So, when Melody's birthday come around I wanted to make a big splash, show up with every kind of present there was, really hot shot, ace it up in front of Marcy. Instead of asking Bobby for extra, which he would of give me, I forged one of their checks for two hundred and fifty dollars. Dum-dum!

" 'Course I got caught about the check and got my ass kicked out—blew that deal. Bobby would of kept me, but his partner put the nix. Couldn't blame him.

"So, I followed old Mr. Sun down to Miami and changed my luck, hooked up with a rich woman, not old, not young, about forty-three, just shoveled the dirt on her husband."

Vito coughed up a hoarse laugh, ending in a high "Hee . . ." I was getting to recognize this as a sign he was about to share a good one with me.

"Now this Barbara—was her name—this Barbara had a body wouldn't end, slim, tiny waist, great boobies, beautiful thick hair, long rich-lady legs, an ass like two duck eggs in a napkin, but a face—ooeeww! If you saw her walkin' down the street goin' *away* from you—Ma-*donn*'!" He made the Italian finger-shaking gesture. "But, if you saw her *comin' at you*—turn you to stone. A face that would back up a Chinese funeral procession! Oversexed, too, because her old man had been under the sad condition of a stroke for a couple years, so she wasn't gettin' much. That lasted five months, but I screwed up there, too. But that was *her* fault. For the main reason, she was embarrassed in public.

"Funny, the men, they was all proud as peacocks to have me around. The women, the three I hooked up with, they was embarrassed in public. The women was always planning a—ah, you know, like a *ruse*—is that right?"

"Yes." (Youse and ruse!)

A pugnacious sliver in his voice: "See, I know a word or two! More than you'd think, I bet." Then: "Yeah, you know, ruses as to why you was there. You were building shelves, or driving their car, or fixing the plumbing. The women were chintzier, too. No, that's wrong, the women weren't chintzy in that they didn't spend it on you, they just never wanted you to have enough cash to get a block away on your own."

Vito looked at me, then asked: "What are youse smiling about?"

I realized I'd been smiling all along at him. "Why do you say 'youse' sometimes and sometimes you don't?"

"How do I know? I know the difference. I know, if I stop to think, that 'youse' ain't right." He laughed. "See, I know about ain't, too. It's just, you learn it when you're a kid, it sticks with you. Habit. So—don't tell me *that's* what you were smiling about?"

"No."

"So—what?"

"I'm getting a kick out of you," I told him, in all honesty. "Also, I'm high, for the first time in my life and it feels good."

"Good, I'm glad you feel good. You—like you had a bitch of a day, didn't you?" He held up a finger. "See, I didn't say 'youse.' "

I laughed. "Yes."

"What's so funny?" he asked.

"I don't know, the whole *thing* seems funny now." I suddenly let out a whoop. "*Thank Christ in heaven!*"

We both laughed for a good long while, not howling gales, just easy rolling laughter. I wasn't even sure what we were laughing about, but it seemed like a good idea at the time.

When we wound down, I asked: "Didn't it mix you up, hooking up with both sexes? Wasn't it confusing?"

"Naw, what's the big deal? Why does it have to be one? You know what to do with each and you do it, if you want, or you don't. Now me, I never hooked up with real fruity types, the ones with the wrists. Un-uh! You wanna go to bed with a man, go to bed with a man. Same with a woman. You want to make it with a woman, pick a real woman, a femme. That's always been my motto. I couldn't get it up with a real fruity type. The sexes both got their good points, but they aren't interchangeable with the bodies, if you get my theme."

"Which were the best sex?"

Vito blinked his eyes in serious contemplation. "Mmn, I gotta level, the men and the women were just about equally good. Anyone goes out of his way, puts out, to get sex, likes sex, that it means that much to them—they're usually pretty good at it. They was all good sex, most of 'em. Good sex looks for good sex, they know where to find it. They sniff it out. 'Course some got their Ph.D. at the game and some don't. I tell you, this Barbara I was tellin' you about, for pure technique—oh, she was a roller coaster, give you a ride would take the starch out of you for a week. She was extra good 'cause she was makin' up with her body for her face. Anyhow, that's mostly the way it went, this one and that."

He seemed to be finished talking; I was hoping he wasn't because I was feeling dreamy and relaxed and he was better than any movie I'd seen since *Gone with the Wind*.

Then a bolt of energy struck him. "See, I would always screw it up. Mostly the lyin' thing would get me in trouble. And funny, I didn't lie about big things, mostly little things. Just to make the day, you know, a little lighter for me. But people don't dig bein' lied to."

"Couldn't you stop?"

"Couldn't, couldn't, couldn't, *couldn't!* I'd lied to save my skin from my old man, my old lady, my brothers and sisters, since I was a polliwog. I could not stop lying!

"Another thing, I think I already told you. I was a moron with a buck, when it came my way, zingo, right through the fingers. An easy touch, anyone asked me, if *I* had it, *they* had it. I don't mean to brag, but I always been generous when I had it. But see, when I *didn't* have it, I'd do dumb things to get it. Little thefts, deal in hash, pot, acid. I got caught once, they threw me in the slammer."

"*Slammer?*"

"Yeah, the cooler, jail, seven months! Dumb—Christ, I get a diploma for dumb!" Then a sigh, and a knuckle crack. "But some good times I had, too. I lived in Paris, France, that was with Richard, for eight months. *Voulez-vous couchez avec moi?*"

"Wouldn't you know that one!"

He crossed his eyes at me. "Also, see, another reason I was dumb. Listen, get this, I *kept* myself dumb. Once I started hustlin' the bones, I was always with people a hundred times smarter than me. I mean, I ran around with people who were people, not trash like me. But—way I figured, I could never learn what they knew. Christ, it would take me a century to catch up, so I played it the other way. I played it like a tough little wop who also happened to swing. They'd get a kick out of my lingo. I'd go to a party at Fire Island or the Hamptons or Connecticut or Bucks County, I'd be the toughest, the scroungiest one there."

He grinned, held up a finger, and said, "People dig that, they do. Lots of people can't get it up with people on the same level as them. They can only make it with scroungies, trade. It excites them, they figure they don't gotta compete with another brain. They're just doin' it with—like an animal. True, it turns them on. I knew it, so I played it that way. I'd be—oh, I'd be very unique. Vivid. I got attention. So I never tried to change anything, not even the way I talked. I had it workin' for me, so I kept it. You make out for yourself by certain little iggies, you don't throw 'em away."

Vito slapped the butcher block with the palm of his hand and sounded one of his donkey-bray *hee*'s. "Jesus, I get wound up when I'm high, don't I?"

"Go ahead, I feel like listening."

"You do? Truth? If you wanta rap, I'll take a breather."

"No, you—go ahead. Goddamnit, I want to know about Ben."

Vito looked at me and slipped on his wise face, which consisted of half-lowered lids over cat eyes and slightly pursed mouth. "Youse can't *imagine* Ben and me lovers, can you?"

A short burst of laughter from Vito. "I tell this one better untied." When I remained silent, he added, "You want to let me up so we can talk like adults?"

"No, Vito." I gave him a large plastic grin. "See, I'm getting to dig you so much, I just don't want to take the chance of losing you."

"Mmnn . . . you're a pisser, Mr. Zoole! Okay. Summer before last, I'd just racked myself out of my latest deal. So, bein' in between hookups, I took a job as waiter at this fancy restaurant run by two rich dykes in Southampton. Both very jazzy, zippy-looking, great dressers. You wouldn't even *know* they was dykes until you caught 'em drunk at their house about three A.M. Then you'd think they was John Wayne and George C. Scott, which is actually what we called 'em. Oh, not to their faces, un-uh. Could they throw some vivid punches, used to womp the shit out of each other.

"One Saturday night late, about a quarter to eleven, party of about twelve, mixed, not gay, comes in, and Ben was one of them."

"Did you know who he was?"

"No, I didn't know my ass then. I didn't even know who Norman Mailer was even. But I spotted Ben for a hump right off the bat. They all ordered dinner. Now this restaurant was very pissy, soak you eighteen-twenty bucks apiece to get outta there alive. Ben ordered poulet almond—almond chicken, right? I take the order to the kitchen, it's so late the cook's out of it. Get this, I'm all dolled up, black pants, red sash, white shirt, black tie and little red monkey jacket, so I come back to the table and give him the word. 'I'm sorry, eighty-six on the bird.' 'What?' he asked, he's laughin'. 'The chicken is eighty-sixed,' I tell him. Even though he's a writer he never heard of it. Eighty-six the chicken means we're out of it. Jesus, he laughed for about five minutes. The whole table laughed. They were all oiled anyhow. So I clowned up the rest of the meal for 'em.

"Like, this one lady ordered duck à l'orange. Happens the duck wasn't so good this night. It was greasy, so I said, "Un-uh, I'd cool it with the quack-quack.' 'Why?' she asks. 'It's wearing too much of that greasy kid stuff,' I told her. And on like that. If I had a table of live ones, I'd usually sneak on a little show for 'em, then I could count on a good tip.

"This night I got a *fifty-dollar tip*! When they left I hadda hunch I'd see Ben again. Get this, just as John Wayne and me were closin' up, about a quarter to two, Ben comes back for a nightcap, alone. So we blah-blah a little; I can tell he thinks I'm a boot in the ass. Kismetville, next day I'm shopping for George C. Scott in Southampton and I bump into him in the hardware store. *Son* of Kismet, two days later I see him on the beach, that's when we really connected."

Vito snapped his fingers. "Two *weeks* later I took off on the big bird with him for Malibu, California, to take care of him and his house while he started on a new book. He really dug me. Jesus, what a guy! Talk about vivid."

Vito shook his head, paused for a long time, as if re-creating him. "Great-looking, really great-looking, dark-brown eyes, huge brown eyes would stab you right in the heart. And a man, all man, no matter what he did. He swung both ways since he was fourteen and no matter which way he swung, he swung hard. Forty-six when he died, but he looked no more than thirty-five—not even. He wasn't all that famous, except for that one book."

"*Remember When We Were All Lovers?*"

"Yeah," Vito said, delighted that I knew of it. "Yeah—you read it?"

"Yes, it was a beautiful book."

"I'm glad you read it. Hey, would you believe that's the first book I ever read? Oh, I'd peeked inside a few but that's the first whole book I ever read. How about that for dumb?"

"Have you read any others?"

An immediate hurt look. "Sure, what do you think? I read all of Ben's, six altogether, four of 'em I didn't understand—truth. That's okay, Ben said nobody else understood 'em either. Then I read *Catcher in the Rye, Midnight Cowboy*—Ben made me a list to break me in so I wouldn't get turned off reading—an old book, *King's Row*. And *Papillon*. Hey, I even wrote a little poem once, when I was high, only a couple of lines but Ben dug it. Wanna hear?"

"Shoot."

Vito cleared his throat, then allowed for a small dramatic pause before speaking:

"Oh, to go home, but where?
never yet was there."

"I like it, too," I told him.

"Ben liked it, too. When I told him I was gonna write *my* book, *Tough Shit! The Story of My Life So Far*, I was kidding naturally. But he said if I had a brain in my head I really would, write it all down, all my experiences, just like I talk. I was gonna actually do it when we got to Mexico."

"Mexico?"

"Yeah, see he finished his first draft of his book in Malibu, and he decided to get away from so many people he knew, so he could really wind it up. We was gonna live in Mexico for six months. On the beach, down in the Yucatan part.

"First I gotta tell you, we used to take walks along the beach almost every afternoon, the greatest walks. Then is when we'd rap serious, along about sunset. I told Ben all about my life and he understood what made my springs rust. The main part, he wanted to help me. He had this program all mapped out to dummy me up.

"The way he put it—so, okay, be a card, talk funny, have your own little bag of tricks, be the life of the party. Great at twenty-six, twenty-seven, twenty-eight. But then, he said, you're gonna wake up one morning and—flash, you're forty. Four-oh! Then you'll find out that what you are is just a dumb stupid-ass schmuck that everyone's tired of, *and* your line of chatter, *and* you don't know your ass from your mouth, the buns have fallen, you can only get your pecker up when the moon's full and suddenly people—oh, suddenly people aren't any more knockin' you down on the street and draggin' you home for patticakes. And that's the only reason they'd *take* you home because you're a dumb schmuck that can't talk about anything else, or *do* anything else.

"Oh, he laid that one on me more than once. At first he hurt me. I knew it was true, but hearing it straight on from someone you really dig—it spooked me. So he had this program of reading, listening to music—Mahler, I got turned on to Mahler something fierce. He can really draw the water outta me. Especially that Number Four. Anyhow, Ben said besides reading and all that, what I really had to start doing was—*thinking*. That I had to learn how to use my brain before it got petrified from *dis*-use. He used to tell me: 'Vito, if you could only learn how to use your brain half as well as you use your pecker, you got nothin' to worry about.' "

Vito reflected on the truth of this for a moment. "Jesus, the lying thing! Oh, how he hated that! And Ben could spot 'em before they was outta my mouth. One time he caught me red-handed, a little thing, tiny, but you'd have thought it was the end of the world.

"I knew he wanted to catch *Five Easy Pieces*, which he'd never seen. Me either. But he was having a good day at the machine. Rainy day, so I told him I'd take in another movie, 'cause we was planning to see it together. I zip off to Santa Monica but the only movie I really want to see is *Five Easy Pieces*. So I go. I dig it, I can easy see it twice, so just to keep everything smooth, when I get home I tell him I saw some other movie, I forget which, some dog.

"Zap—two nights later we go to this big dinner party up the beach in Malibu, and someone starts rapping about *Five Easy Pieces*. I chime right in blah-blah-blah-blah-blah-blah-blah-blah-blah"— Vito punctuated with the raspberry sound—"about how the best part was when the guy cleared off the table in the diner with one swipe of his arm and, suddenly, I feel, I don't see, 'cause he's in back of me at the bar, but I *feel* these eyes burning a hole right through my head. I turn around. Like flamethrowers, they was.

"Ben says very quietly, 'Vito, come here, step outside on the deck a minute.' I walk over and as we're going out the door, he turns to the crowd, about fifteen people, and he says, 'I'm gonna beat the shit out of this chronic lying little bastard—in case anyone wants to watch.' Without another peep he yanks me outside and knocks me off the deck for openers, then he jumps down on the sand and beats the crap outta me! Everyone standing on the deck *with drinks* watching—the fuckin' *floor show!* When he gets through he says, 'Vito, every time I catch you lying I'm gonna give you a repeat performance. So—for your own sake, either stop it, take judo lessons, or pack up and ship out!' "

"So, did you stop?"

"Almost. I mean he really beat on me. After that, I'd really stop and *think* before I'd open the mouth."

Once more I glanced out of the window. Still the snow fell. I walked over to look down at the street. The snow had covered all tracks by now; not one footstep or tire mark to be seen. I turned to Vito. "How come I don't feel silly any more? Where did the silliness go?"

"It passes, you get quiet, then you pick up on something, a word or a sentence or just a name strikes you and you're off and runnin'. Then you get hungry, usually for sweets, then *most people* get horny, not knock-down, drag-out hot-nuts horny, just nice and cuddly horny." Again the pursed mouth, the closest he got to camp. "*Most* people, that is. Then you get sleepy and that's it, the works. Pot is really the kittens."

My mouth was dry; I did have a yen. "Now that you mention it. I could go for some ice cream."

"Yeah!" Vito shouted, "it's working. Ice cream now, horny next."

I laughed. "You want some? Ice cream, that is?"

"Do I want some! I told you I ain't had nothin' to eat. Christ, I'm so hungry I could eat the asshole out of a dead wolf!"

"Classy!"

"Yeah, Ben used to get a kick out of that, too."

I went to the freezer, got out the ice cream, and found a jar of fudge sauce. While I fixed our sundaes, Vito discoursed on the theory of his sexual activities. "See, a lot of it was done just for company. I mean that for serious, no copout. Once I got used to being with people that were people, not animals, I dug it. Well, how was I gonna get decent, educated people to sit down and have a conversation with me? I wasn't. I wasn't gonna sit on any park bench in Central Park and shoot a little amiable shit with Teddy Kennedy or Norman Mailer or Shirley MacLaine. But if I went to *bed* with them—"

"You've been to bed with Teddy Kennedy and Norman Mailer and Shirley MacLaine?"

"Hah, hah, very funny! You know what I mean. I was just using them for examples. I tell you, though, Ben says he thought Norman Mailer would *like* to do it with a guy. Probably he would like to have it be rape, with a gun at his head, so he'd *have* to, but then he'd dig it. That's why all that big deal machismo crap he gives out.

Or else he'd want it to be some big deal judo-wrestling match, but he'd sneak in a little orgasm and call it sweat! Hah! Oh, yeah, I've known my share of *those* types. Anyhow—you see, you got me off the track with your wise-ass—what I meant was, if I went to bed with someone, then they *had* to talk with me. Before we did it, they sure had to, sometimes even during, and after, too."

I handed Vito his fudge sundae. "Here—Happy New Year."

"Thanks." He looked down into the bowl. "Umn, I could digest this a lot better sittin' up."

"Try it in this position," I told him. As I watched him dive into it and, as I dived into mine, I realized I could not keep him tied down much longer, I didn't really want to. Still, maybe it was the pot that guided my feelings. Again, it was his *surprises* that triggered apprehension at the idea of setting him free. It would only figure he'd have one more up his sleeve once he was untied. I wondered if all his talk was merely spilled out to con me, to charm me. Had he given me the clue time and again by stressing his penchant for lying?

The most worrisome item on the list, however, was this: I was beginning to feel something very much akin to affection for this character, Vito Antenucci. I felt about him not unlike the way I'd felt toward Bobby Seale. Christ only knows they had points in common. From Vito's description, his education and family background were about on a par with Bobby's. Both were scroungy outlaws, both were suckers for affection—Vito was, I knew this—both lived by their wits, such as they were.

I regarded Vito with warmth; I didn't like owning up to it, but I did.

Didn't anything turn out the way it was supposed to? No, not a job, not Kate; nothing seemed, in the end, to make sense.

I could not even catch a burglar without botching it up.

There was not much talk while we devoured the ice cream. Only the sound of spoon in bowl. After we'd finished, I asked Vito: "Were you with Ben when he died?"

"With him, was I ever with him! Yeah . . . oh, yeah." Vito remained silent and I thought that was all I would get from him. Finally he spoke. "Three weeks before we was leaving for Mexico. On a Tuesday. Ben worked all morning, played tennis in the afternoon, came home around four. We went for a long walk, then we took a swim, a good long swim. When we dried off and come back to the house there was this sunset takin' place, like the end of the world. Knock your eyes out. We—ah, we decided to make it. A friend of mine had just got me a new box of poppers and I—"

"Poppers? What are poppers?"

His tone was incredulous. "Poppers, you don't know what are poppers?"

"I guess I've heard the name, but I don't really know what they are."

"Poppers is amyl nitrite, little yellow capsules. People with heart trouble sniff 'em if they're having a bummer with their pump. But—Jesus, you never heard of poppers for *sex*? You break this little capsule, put it in a Benzidrex inhaler, and sniff it."

"When?"

"When you're makin' it, off and on during, and then a major whiff right when you're ready to put the icing on the cake."

I had to smile. "What does it do?"

"Blows your mind, makes your sense of touch and feel and concentration on the doin's at hand magnified about a hundred times. I talked to a doctor once, something about it rushes all this oxygen in. I don't know, but it works. And when you finally blast off, makes it seem like it's in Technicolor, wide-screen, stereophonic sound, *and* slow motion. Feels like it's lasting about five solid minutes. Not just a little spurt, squirt—a real gusher.

"Anyhow, I'd got this new box and—Ben, now Ben *liked* them but not all the time, said it wasn't good to depend on 'em to make the scene. Which he was right, it isn't. Also, there was rumors too much sniffin' could cause a blowout of a blood vessel up in the attic, too. When I took them out this afternoon, Ben said no, we didn't need them. 'But Ben,' I said, 'Jesus, look at the *sunset*.' So he said okay—"

"I don't get it."

"It was always great with him, but some times it was all goin' on up in Heaven and the sunset just made me want it to take place in Heaven this afternoon. So we—we used two, maybe three—and we shot up to the Moon and over to Mars and Venus and then we hit Heaven head on. Bammo! Oh, what a winner! Cigars all around.

"After, we were just laying there trying to refocus the eyes, and Ben, he joked, he was breathing so hard and he said, "Oi, Doctor, get a priest.' And we laughed and then calmed down and just lay there. After a while I got up from the bed and I said, 'I'll get a towel.' 'Okay,' Ben said, 'get the little yellow one.' There was this little pale yellow towel we used to keep in a drawer near the bed, only the laundry had just come back fresh and it was in the cabinet in the john down the hall.

"I went into the bathroom and pee'd and washed up—and all that. Then I got the towel, the little yellow one, and walked back to the bedroom. The sun had took a complete powder by this time. It was pretty dark and Ben was lying there, quietly, on his back. I said his name, like from a few yards away. He didn't answer. I figured let him sleep while I start dinner.

"So, into the kitchen, avocado vinaigrette, baked chicken breasts, got 'em all in the works. About seven, I fixed him a rum and diet cola and turned on the TV. He always watched the evening news.

"I went back to the bedroom and I said, 'Hey, Ben, come on, it's wrist-slitting time.' I called it that because Ben would always pass a remark how depressing the news was every night. When he didn't answer, I jiggled him, you know, like put a hand on his leg, which was under the quilt, and gave him a little jiggle. When he still didn't answer, I turned on the bedside lamp.

"He was in the same position but I noticed right away his—those brown eyes were wide open and his—one hand was reaching back, holding on to one of the brass bed rails in back of his head. I walked over close and I said his name, 'Ben.' Once, twice, three times. His eyes didn't blink, nothin'. I—then I touched him, put the back of my hand up by his neck, then his cheek. He was already very— cool. Hardly, it wasn't hardly an hour and he was already—"

Vito stopped speaking. Neither one of us spoke for a very long time. Eventually, a tiny sigh, like a bubble, escaped Vito's lips. He cleared his throat. "You know what I always wondered? Still, even to this day, I wonder if he called out, maybe when I was peeing or when the toilet was flushing and—and I didn't hear him? Or did he even *know* it was happening? Or what? If he cried out, if it was *hurting* him—and I didn't hear because I was *peeing!* Oh, wouldn't that be the height of tacky?"

"Yes, I guess it would."

Vito shook his head. " 'I'll get a towel.' 'Okay, get the little yellow one.' " He turned to look at me. "Would you ever, if you ever *thought* about it, would you ever imagine those would be the last things two people would say to each other? Jesus! 'I'll get the towel.' 'Okay, get the little yellow one.' "

Vito glanced down at his hands and gave his knuckles a workout. "Talk about your spins. Oh . . . Oh-ho!"

"You took the blame?"

"Whether or not, the doctor—he was a friend of Ben's, too—said, you know, forty-six, tennis, swimming, we'd always jog for part of our walk, then sex, poppers—who knows? But, oh, yeah, I took the blame, all the little fuck-ups in my life leading up to the one big King Kong."

Vito abruptly shook his head, as if he were shaking off spider webs. "Hey, let's light up another. Talk about heavy! Thud, thud. I didn't mean to get so heavy. Okay?"

"Okay."

Vito handed me the third joint. I lighted it, took a puff, and we smoked, passing it back and forth.

"Truth, Jimmy, the most ashamed I ever was of my whole self, ever, and I put in some tacky capers, was the couple of months after Ben died. The biggest mess you ever saw, that was me. I took to the sewers. I don't even remember half the things I did. Which is good, I guess. But—drunk and pot and LSD and drunk again and crying—oh, the water pouring out. And then the hard stuff, and I knew if I stuck around California it was curtains, so I came back East. Also I had got in a little trouble out there. I could hear the slammer calling.

"But, you see, I was thumbs down on the world—account of Ben. Oh, I fuckin' hated the world and every miserable bastard in it. Thumbs down on the whole gang. Comin' East didn't help. I just couldn't climb out of the sewer. Mainly I think because I couldn't be alone, couldn't *sleep* alone for the dark thoughts. I been playin' with a bunch of rats, 'cause rats is who you meet when you hang out in the sewer. I got kicked out of my last pad. I was semihooked up with this rat, a humpy rat, but a rat."

Vito's eyes flicked to me, he glanced down at the pillow in front of him, poked it with his finger. "So I was wondering"—his eyes returned to me—"could I spend the night?"

I focused closely on him, tied down, bare-assed, completely helpless, to see if he was for real. He was, his forehead was creased and his large blue-green eyes were wide open seriously waiting for an answer to his question.

All I could manage was "*Could you*—" before I spun off into convulsions of laughter. At first Vito was uncomprehending. His look of total confusion only hypoed my laughter. This, added to the dizzying effects of our latest smoke, had me so weakened I could only howl—attempts at speech were mere gargles—howl again and point to him.

Eventually, directed by my gestures, he glanced back over his shoulder at his bare, most untenable position. In a second it dawned upon him and he joined me. Soon the two of us were gibbering fools.

Tears dripped from Vito's eyes. After a while, in his position, it was also uncomfortable to sustain such a prolonged bout of laughter without being able to move. I'd started out sitting in the easy chair. I was now half out of it, hands clutching my stomach, sliding to the floor, my heels scuffing the rug.

Vito waved me away, able only to gasp, "Cramps!" I laughed all the more. Now he was not only tied down, bare-bottomed, but he had the cramps. When I was able not only to put words together but to deliver them, I said: "Could you *spend the night*? You can't even go to the *bathroom!*"

Vito managed to hold his breath while he gasped, "Guy, I meant to tell you, *I did, in the sink, while you was gone!*"

That was the capper, we were off again, howling with laughter, so much so that we heard nothing, no footsteps, not even the door being opened.

We were only aware we were no longer alone when we heard the sound of laughter, other than our own. I believe Vito and I heard it together, because we both turned toward the front door at the same time.

Carmine stood inside the front door. Two other men flanked him. Carmine was laughing—head thrown back, mouth open, showing the glint of gold fillings in his molars—and pointing at Vito. The other two grinned, but they were not laughing. I had forgotten about Carmine and his sudden appearance made me laugh all the more.

I glanced at Vito. He had, in these few seconds, almost stopped laughing entirely. The look in his eyes told me more than anything that he was not pleased at the arrival. I felt a moment's annoyance at the abrupt change in his attitude.

All three were in costume; to my eyes, this added to the hilarity. Carmine, dressed as a South American gaucho, wore black boots, black gaucho pants, white shirt, bolero jacket, and the classic broad-brimmed black hat with leather strap beneath the chin. Carrying a black leather tote bag slung over his shoulder, he made a dashing José Greco–ish appearance with his one silver earring. The sight of *him* was not especially funny.

The shorter of the other two, a compact rugged fellow, his jet-black hair brush-cut, was dressed as Batman in long red underwear, over which he wore a black bikini cut in the shape of a bat. A black cape topped his outfit. His underwear was baggy and this, together with his size, made him a more likely candidate for Mighty Mouse than Batman.

The third was gotten up as a motorcyclist: black boots, crushed cap, a galaxy of studs and chains decorating the basic black of his leather pants and jacket. He, of the three, appeared demented. He was far too beefy for the outfit and his tired face sagged all gray and pudgy beneath the ridiculous crushed cap. Way over the hill to be cavorting as a Hell's Angel, he would have made a better, aging, rococo cupid as long as he had to play dress-up. My immediate reaction was: back to wardrobe!

Again I glanced at Vito; for a second his eyes flicked to me, then back to them. There was no humor in them. This surprised me because I was feeling fuzzy and lightheaded and the sight of this trio struck me funny.

They shook the snow off and stamped their feet; none of them wore overcoats. There was something about their eyes, a kind of dilated opaqueness, that indicated they were well into something besides booze.

Carmine walked toward us; the closer he came the more he laughed. I did, too. I knew we were laughing at the same thing: the incongruity of this sight in view of his assessment of me. The other two straggled behind him.

When he was only a few steps away from Vito, he slapped his hand against his thigh and, speaking through his laughter, said: "Jimmy—you're into *my* scene—oh, Jimmy!" He laughed again. "Jimmy, Jimmy, Jimmy!" Then: "Oh, you're a fox, all the time we worked together, what—six, seven months? You played it so square, so *square!*"

I'd gotten up from the easy chair by this time. Vito lay stretched out between Carmine and me. Carmine turned to his buddies.

"Clark Kent we used to call him!" He looked back at me and shook his head. "That girl, Christ, couldn't get you out for a Coke without her. And now—look at this! When you come out of the closet you really—CHARGE!"

He stepped up to Vito, reached down and smacked him on the ass. "What a crazy rumble seat!"

"Hands off the merchandise!" Vito snapped.

Cocking his head, Carmine looked at him closely. "I've seen you someplace . . ."

"Yeah," Vito said, his voice tough and challenging. "I seen you, too!" Vito turned to me. "The bunch of 'em, I seen 'em, The Unholy Three, they call 'em at the Ankle-Strap." Vito glanced behind Carmine at the other two. "I also seen better drag on French poodles!"

Carmine took it in good humor. "Peppy, too. That's right, the Ankle-Strap." He whacked Vito's ass again. "I never forget a pretty face."

The other two laughed. Carmine made the introductions. The short, compact one was Pidgeon, the motorcyclist was Stanley. Indicating Vito, Carmine asked, "Does it have a name?"

"Yes, Vito," I told him.

Pidgeon stepped up closer. "Yeah, it's that little wop from the Ankle-Strap."

Now it was the motorcycle's turn. "Sure, I remember him. He'd cruise anything: dogs, cats, wallpaper—doorknobs!"

Vito quickly looked up at me to catch my reaction to this slur. There was concern in his eyes and I liked him for it. I did not like Pidgeon or Stanley.

"Yeah," Vito said, "anything but chubbos, I ain't no chubby chaser!"

Carmine laughed. "You tell 'em, Vito." Carmine looked across Vito to me. "So, Jimmy—all this time, I always had eyes for you and you swinging away like crazy *all this time*."

There was an unhealthy scent to them. I was suddenly not so sure I wanted them there.

"I got your message from Sammy. Tried to call but—busy. Tried again from Ginny's, busy again, the operator checked"—Carmine glanced around, spotted the phone—"off the hook. That's not nice, leave a message to call, then take the phone off the hook."

"Carmine, honest, I completely forgot."

"No big deal." Carmine sighed and flashed a smile. "We're all together now." I did not like the sound of that. Carmine turned to his friends. "Didn't I tell you he was a pussycat?"

It seemed, with the three of them lined up on the other side of Vito, like an extremely good idea to let him up. I reached down to untie the backstrap. "What are you doing?" Carmine asked.

"Look, he's a friend of mine and—"

He cut me off. "A friend? I should hope a friend!"

"I mean—the joke's over, he's been tied up for hours."

Carmine placed a restraining hand on my arm. "Ah-ah, leave it, looks nice all laid out on display."

I tried to loosen the knot. "Carmine, come on, we'll have a drink, maybe smoke a little—"

He gave my hands a brisk slap. I laughed, I don't know why. I was feeling the effects of our last joint and wishing we hadn't smoked it. When I kept my hold on the straps, Carmine walked around the front of the butcher block to where I stood. "Leave it!"

"I want to let him up."

He shoved me away. A ripple of dizziness hit me. I stumbled back against the kitchen table and knocked a small sauce-pan to the floor. I bent down to pick it up but the move increased my dizziness. I straightened up and put a hand to my forehead.

"Jimmy," Carmine said, "you called, left a message, then when I show up—the joke's *over*?"

"Carmine, I know it looks funny, all this, but I don't—like you said—swing. I don't."

Carmine roared at this. "Don't—you *don't*! Christ, you're a hoot on top of it. Can barely walk you're so stoned and"—he pointed to Vito—"what's *that*? Don't tell me that's your normal everyday New Year's Eve centerpiece?"

"Carmine, I know it looks—"

"Looks!" Carmine whooped. "What were the two of you doing—having a Tupperware Party?"

For some odd turned-on reason the phrase struck me funny and I laughed. Although even while I was laughing I had a suspicion there was nothing all that funny. Carmine laughed, so did the other two.

I often have the actor's recurrent nightmare. I suddenly find myself onstage opening night of a Broadway play—only to realize I haven't rehearsed, don't know my lines, don't even know the plot of the play or how I happened to get involved. I wonder how I possibly could have gotten as far as opening night without this knowledge and appeal to my fellow actors for help, for a clue. No one gives it, everyone is frantically busy with his own problems.

I found myself in a similar situation now. I was ill prepared for this scene. I knew there must be some way to slip out of it, but I could not for the life of me think of any appropriate lines. In the meantime I kept laughing over—Tupperware Party.

This pleased Carmine and he walked over to me. "That's better, relax, we'll have some fun, put it all together." He reached out, placing his hands on my waist and squeezing. My high degree of ticklishness pleased him even more. He looked over his shoulder at the other two and said, "No, Christ, they don't swing, do they?"

Stanley and Pidgeon both echoed: "No, oh, no!" They laughed now, too, along with Carmine. So did I, even as I squirmed to get away.

"Is the Pope Catholic?" Carmine said.

"Does a bear shit in the woods?" Pidgeon asked.

I broke away from Carmine several steps into the living-room area. He was right after me, grabbing me from behind, his arms around my waist.

"Carmine—listen, this is crazy, we *worked* together!"

"So now we play together. All work and no play make Jimmy a dull boy!"

Carmine lifted me off the floor and swung me around just as I saw Pidgeon step up to the sink and reach underneath Vito's stomach to grab him. "Let's see what he's got here."

Vito cried out; Pidgeon had not grabbed him gently.

"Leave him alone! Jesus, you pigs!" I shouted this, wrenching myself away from Carmine at the same time. "Get out of here!" I wheeled around to face Carmine. "Carmine, get them out of here!"

"Oh-ho . . ." This, a warning sound from Carmine. "So that's the way it is. You already got your jollies and now the fun's over, is that it?"

He came at me just as I heard Vito cry out, "Let's go, you fuckin' creep!" I swung at Carmine; he dodged and the punch landed ineffectively on his shoulder. He grabbed me, wrestled me around, and finally got his arms around my waist again, pinning my arms inside his and dragging me toward the bed.

"Vito—Jesus, help me!" The hopelessness of my cry for help struck me as the words came out. Nevertheless as I fought to get away from Carmine, I called out again: "Vito!"

I heard his voice. "Leave him alone, you creepy bastards, he's stoned!"

Carmine flipped me down on the bed and threw himself on top of me, straddling my chest and pinning me down. He was breathing hard and laughing again. "I don't mind a little work to get it, not at all!"

Again I saw his gold molars, only this time the view was too close. He was lowering his face toward mine. "Carmine, *don't!*" He kept laughing, even as he pressed his mouth down on mine. He'd used some sort of breath sweetener and I got a sickening blast of it.

Then, as I twisted with all my strength to get away from him, my elbow cracked him solidly in the jaw. His head jerked up and away from me. He was stunned for a split second. He shook his head, clearing his vision, then our eyes locked and I didn't avert mine when I spoke. "Jesus, you dirty pig!"

He slapped me hard on the side of the head. My vision blurred.

"You little cock-teaser! You want to play rough, is that what you like? I bet you do! Hold him!"

The other two took over, pinning me down, as Carmine stood up and dug into his tote bag. I put up what struggle I could, but it was useless against the two of them, then the three of them, as he quickly bound my feet and wrists with leather straps.

No contest, there I was. My shirt was ripped, my shoes were off, but my pants were still on. This was the least of my worries. Once I was trussed up, the three of them pulled away and stood looking down at me. They all breathed heavily. Pidgeon and Stanley were grinning. Not Carmine.

While I was hating myself more than them, for starting the whole asinine thing, a total nonsequitur struck me. Lying there on my back, securely bound, I thought: *I want out*—want out of acting! The helplessness of my position, at that very instant, was the same helplessness I so often felt as an actor. A strange spinoff at an even stranger time, but there it was. I was juggling this around in my mind when Carmine reached up and felt his jaw.

"I'm sorry—I—"

"Skip it," Carmine said. It was not the kind of skip it one wants to hear.

Despite this, my mood abruptly changed. "I lied, I'm not sorry!"

"What?" Stanley asked, threateningly, playing big man for Carmine.

"You!" I shouted up at him. "You look like an asshole tied in the middle!"

Vito laughed.

I appreciated his laughter but I was suddenly in a rage that they'd invaded our New Year's.

Stanley stepped toward me, hand raised. "Leave him alone," Carmine said. "I'll take care of him." He glanced down at me. "Won't I, Jimmy?"

No one spoke for a moment. I was further stunned, not as much by the struggle or Carmine's slap—I could still feel the sting—as by the perverse insanity of my predicament. I remember thinking: no, this isn't possible, after everything else—*I'm not going to get raped!*

Add 'em up, Bobby!

Vito's croupy laughter broke the silence. The three of them turned to look at him. So did I. I could not see his head from my position, only his legs and feet.

Vito spit his words out: "Serves you right, you prick!"

I could not believe him.

Carmine laughed and uttered a knowing "Ah-*hah*!" The other two snickered along with him.

"Hey, Carmine," Vito said, in his wisest voice, "I'll make you a deal."

Carmine did not reply, simply looked at him with eyebrows raised.

Vito only said, "Eh, Carmine?"

"Yeah . . . ?" Carmine replied. He was not rushing into anything.

"If you like to tie 'em up, I'll bet you like a good show, too. Don't you? I mean, a real freaky show?"

Carmine glanced down at me, back to Vito. He took his time, then shrugged. "Who doesn't?"

Vito laughed. "You like to watch? I'll bet you do." When Carmine didn't reply, Vito said, "Everyone likes to watch." He used Carmine's words. "*Who doesn't*—right?" Carmine had elected to play it cool. "Okay," Vito said, "I'll make you a deal. If you give me first dibs on"—his tone was toughly facetious—"my *pal, Jimmy!* I'll make you a trade."

"What kind of trade?" Carmine asked.

"I'll give you four ounces of hash. Pure hash, the best stuff, straight from Tangiers."

"Four ounces of hash?" Pidgeon asked.

"Yeah, a four-ounce hunk, one great piece. You know how much it's worth an ounce? Pure hash?"

"Where is it?" Carmine asked.

"I got it. Let me up and I'll give it to you." When Carmine hesitated, Vito snickered. "Jesus, there's three of you and one of me, bare-ass! What am I gonna try? I'll make you an even trade, four ounces of pure hash for a go at—*my buddy there!*" He hit the words hard. "Come on, we can all turn on, have a party. You can watch all you want." He shrugged. "I dig it. Truth."

Stanley laughed, a simple moronic sort of laugh, and said, "Ey, Carmine?"

There was a long pause before Carmine shrugged and turned to Pidgeon. "Let him up."

Pidgeon and Stanley went to Vito and untied him. He slid off the sink unit slowly. "Jesus, I'm stiff!" Although his shirttails dropped down to cover him, he picked up the bathtowel I'd used to wipe off his face. Turning to me, he grabbed his genitals—now bunched up underneath the shirting—in one hand and with a small shaking gesture, said: "Tit for tat, huh, Jim-may!"

Stanley whistled. Carmine and Pidgeon laughed and looked at me.

The rest happened very fast.

Vito wrapped the towel around his waist, walked to the bed, and knelt down, without as much as a glance. I was hoping he'd give me a wink or some sign that he was kidding. I found it hard to believe he was joining the enemy. He reached under the bed and took out a small airline bag. He had not let me know it was there; this surprise, call it a small deceit even, added to his possible duplicity, both disappointed and worried me.

He stood up, glanced around the room, and walked over to the rolltop desk. Opening the bag, he took from it a small parcel wrapped in brown paper, secured with rubber bands. He slipped the bands off, undid the paper, and from a piece of cellophane took what looked like a small brown rock. "Here yah go . . ." He held it out in his hand.

Carmine walked over and took it; the other two joined him. The three of them stood by a lamp and inspected the piece of hashish.

Vito quickly glanced to his side and scuttled over to the corner of the bookcase. Swooping down toward the floor, he came up with the gun.

The swiftness of his movement caught Carmine's attention. He swung around and automatically took a quick step toward Vito. "What the—?" He stopped abruptly when Vito pointed the gun at him.

Vito wasted no time. "Hold it. Okay, the three of youse, you got the hash, now—out! Get the fuck outta here or someone's gonna get hurt!" He wagged the gun at them. "You think I wouldn't? Try me!"

As I was thinking of the bulletless gun, Vito said: "You think it ain't loaded?" He moved over to the desk, backing them away from it. He pointed to the hunk of raw wood that had been torn out when I'd fired at the phone. "We already had one—accident." He poked his finger in the gash. "What do you think this is?" He scooted over to the bed, picked up Carmine's tote bag and flung it at him. "Now—*move!*"

No one spoke, no one moved either. Vito's voice stepped up to a shout; he sounded tough and deadly serious. "Shag your asses, goddamnit! Come on, the three of youse—out the door!" Still no one took a step. Vito lowered the gun, cocked it, and aimed in the general direction of their feet.

They all flinched; Stanley was the only one who spoke: "Jesus!"

"First shot'll be at your feet, second—*won't!* Out the door, come on!" He moved forward, straight at them.

Carmine backed toward the door, flanked by Pidgeon and Stanley. Vito kept crowding them. "See—I lied. I don't *like* to be watched! Come on, move—*out!*"

Stanley grabbed the door, swung it open, and the three of them backed out. Vito followed them to the hall. I could hear their footsteps going downstairs. After a moment, he shouted after them: "You got the hash so—*don't come back!* Don't try nothing! You do, you'll be fartin' through a hole in your stomach!"

Vito listened until he could hear the front door slam. Then he stepped back in the room, closed the door, and let out a barrage of laughter!

"Hee—those freaks!" He twirled the gun in his fingers, then looked at me, jabbing his chin in the air. "So, how's it feel—Jimmy-baby? Huh?"

Though I didn't consider myself particularly dense as observer of my fellow man, the events so far made such little sense that I could make head or tail of—*nothing*, let alone Vito's true intent.

He stood there with the empty gun in his hand. There might have been amusement behind his eyes, but it was not spread over his face as he regarded me. The towel slackened of its own accord, then dropped from his waist to the floor. His eyes flicked down to it. Looking up at me, he shrugged his shoulders and eyebrows and then smiled. Not a lewd smile, for all that, his shirttails once again covered him.

For a moment I could not help contemplating—what if he were *not* covered. At the gym Pete would often, more to get a rise out of me than anything, say, "Hey, look at the buns on him!" or "Now there's a three-piece set worthy of bronzing!" My face would heighten in color and he would laugh. Once when I blushed he said: "Listen, do you like your own cock?"

"Well, yes," I replied. "I—yes, I like it. I don't *love* it, but I like it. Why?"

"So, what's wrong with admiring someone else's? There are other works of beauty besides yours."

Preferring not to dwell on this area of speculation, I averted my eyes and glanced to the window. Outside the snow still fell, not as thick as before, and the flakes were finer now. I looked at the clock on the mantel. Ten minutes to three. In the distance I could hear the grind and whir of a snowplow.

Vito's eyes remained on me. The bout with Carmine had taken the edge off my high. Exhaustion, residual from the entire day, was setting in fast. I could feel the heaviness in my veins and up in my eyelids. A headache threatened.

Vito walked slowly to the bed. He looked at the gun in his hand, glanced at the door and said, "I'd make a pretty good actor myself— don't you think?"

"Yes . . ."

I lay on my back, the way I'd been left by Carmine and Company. Vito sat on the edge of the bed, only a foot or two from my waist. He stared down at me. I looked him back in the eyes. We held this look for a long while.

Until a small smile stretched Vito's mouth. Glancing down at my chest, where the shirt had been torn open, he reached over and traced a finger down the center. "I always did like that, just that little bit of hair, that nice little line, leading down . . ." When his finger reached my navel, he lifted his hand away.

"So," he sighed, "don't you think you owe me something?"

I didn't reply. What could I say—yes, no, maybe, what do you want? I was not feeling up to pertinent dialogue. Besides, intuition told me to underplay.

"Yeah," Vito said, "I was always a good actor. Did you believe me, what I told you about Ben?"

I had believed him, but I wasn't going to confirm this. When I didn't reply, he asked, "Supposin' I told you I made it up, that I just tricked with him for a one-night stand?"

Still, I didn't answer.

Again we simply looked at each other. I wondered how long this delaying action could stretch. Once more I was struck by Kate's eyes looking down at me from Vito's face. This was no help.

It was his move. The longer we remained locked in eye-to-eye contact, the longer this limbo continued, the more the suspense. And in this suspense, I had to admit, there was excitement. Excitement I chose not to define. Again I summoned forth Pete. He would have shrugged and said: "*Look, what a way to go, you're tied down, you can indulge in a little mano-a-mano with no guilt whatsoever. What could you do, you're helpless?*"

My mind latched on to that, locked on it. It was an out. I almost smiled—from the combination of relief in the expiation of guilt and from the nervous tension that mounted the longer the silence stretched on.

Something to do with pride kept me from averting my eyes from his. It was his move.

He finally made it. Slowly he bent over and lowered his face toward mine. I stayed perfectly still, *inhaling* an impulse to flinch or turn my head.

When he was directly above me, only inches away, so close that my vision became blurred and I could feel the warmth of his breath, I could not help it—I didn't mean to—it was reflex: I quickly turned my head to the side and emitted some small sound.

A beat, no more, and now Vito slapped me on the side of the head, not hard, I could feel a governor on it, but a slap nevertheless.

He was up off the bed and shouting: "Jesus, what?—you thought I was going to—what do you think, I gotta have someone *tied down* to make it with them?" A burst of laughter, bitter and harsh. "Dumb prick, I was just seein' what you'd do. You think I'm that hard up, I have to have someone tied down? You think I'd mortify myself to make it with a person when a person don't want to? Christ, I may be a hustler but I got my pride, too." There was a pause, then: "Jesus Christ, Jim-may"—still he used my name with such familiarity—"dummy up!" He swept a glass off an end table.

After the crash, there was a long silence. I was the one to finally break it. "What do you want me to do—apologize?"

"No—oh, *shit!*" Then he was back over me, quickly untying my hands and feet. "There—you still got your cherry. Go *can* it!"

He was wound up; he walked away, pacing back and forth. I sat up on the bed and thought: *Bad timing is everything.*

"Jesus!" he shouted, then his tone turned snidely biting: "Would it break your balls if I had a drink?"

"No."

"You want one?"

I nodded, then, for an instant, I almost said, *No, no drink!* I wanted nothing. Yes, I wanted to be alone. *Not* being alone, having to arrange it, also, yes, in a way owing this Vito not one but two rounds of thanks, I also felt the need for some independent activity. A drink required less action of me than anything I could think of, so I lay there in silence.

I want out!

Had I said it out loud or thought it? I turned my head to see him getting ice in the kitchen. He didn't look around. I must have thought it. *Out of what?* The impulse I'd felt when I was tied down revisited me in full. I wanted out of being helpless, just as helpless in this acting profession as if I were bound and gagged.

By the time Vito handed me my drink, he'd simmered down. "Well, what the hell—Happy New Year!"

I was surprised to hear, once more, the sound of my laughter.

"How come you laugh?"

"Punchy, I guess."

"Yeah, I can see how you would be." We each drank. He spoke with frowning gravity. "So, no kidding, how do you feel, really?"

I decided I owed him the decency of leveling with him. "You

really want to know? I feel deeply, seriously, intensely, gravely, perilously fucked up right about now. Truth!"

This seemed to register upon him, until I added, "Vito, I really would like to be alone."

He shook his head. "Ah-ah, no way. If you feel that rotten, I couldn't leave you like *that*!"

I laughed again.

"Hey, guy, what do you laugh—when I'm being serious?"

"Vito—look, I have about one quarter of a thimbleful of energy left and I'll burn it up being serious right back at you. Okay?"

"Shoot." He sat down on the bed.

I spoke to myself as much as to him. "I've been an actor for— since I was eighteen. That's twenty years. Twenty years and I have never had a real, true success. I mean, nothing where everybody sat up on their hind legs and said, 'Jesus, look what he's done—can do!" Oh, I've worked, scraped by, TV, industrials, commercials, Off-Broadway, summer stock. But in twenty years I have only been on Broadway four times, that's an average of once in five years. Big career. It has seriously occurred to me tonight—yes, and *was* occurring crazily enough during the hijinks a while ago—that, finally, after twenty years, I just might be in the wrong business!

"That is not a *fun* occurrence. Can you imagine what it's like to be in a business twenty years and never doing anything . . . special in it? That would be like—like being a hustler for twenty years and never 'hooking up' with *anyone* special, like Ben.

"Why haven't I? Jesus, I don't know. Why have I kept on? I don't even know *that*.

"I do know this. I want to do something special sometime in some *one thing*." Vito opened his mouth to speak. "No, wait a minute. My book was special and I think I can write it, in my own special way. I do. The problem is, I have to figure a way to swing it. I have to be alone and read over this last twenty years and hope to Christ I make some sense out of it. Besides just—a bummer. I have to be alone to think. *Comprendo?*"

Vito's reply was unbelievable. "You said I could spend the night."

"Vito!"

"I'll be quiet like a mouse, I wouldn't say a word, I—"

"Vito, I spill out a whole mess of home truths on my entire life and all I get from you is 'You said I could spend the night!' Don't you understand?"

He hunched up his shoulders. "Sure. But—still—listen, you makin' me go because I gave you a rough time? Okay, so I apologize."

"No, that's not it, Vito. I just really need to be alone."

A sudden giggle from him. "Hah, I gotcha, I can't go, not tonight. I got no pants, New Year's Day—stores all closed."

His tenacity, his energy, after all this time! I got up from the bed and went to the closet. I dug around for a corduroy suit, took it out and presented it to him. "Here, Happy New Year."

His expression admitted defeat. "I only need the pants . . ."

"Take the suit, it's too small for me anyhow." From the dresser I took a pair of shorts, then I got his twenty-seven dollars, added fifteen of my own, and held it out to him. "Here, for a room."

He backed away. "I don't want any money from you."

"You have to have—"

"I'll make out!"

"Take it, goddamnit! The twenty-seven was yours anyhow. And the hashish, you gave away your hashish." I stuffed the money in the coat pocket. "There, it's in there."

Vito turned and walked into the bathroom, carrying the clothes and closing the door behind him.

There was relief, just being in the room alone. I stood in the middle looking around. The place was a mess. I'd always scored A in Compulsive Neatness, a trait I didn't particularly admire in myself but one I was stuck with. Now I merely shrugged. Last things last. The kitchen was the biggest mess. I noticed Bobby Seale's water and food dishes on the floor.

My heart took on weight. I'd momentarily forgotten. I found a large shopping bag and put his two dishes in it, also three cans of cat food and a box of catnip. I wandered around the room collecting all his things, his red scratching post, three rubber balls, and an old sock of mine tied into a knot with catnip inside. I even found a book on the care and training of cats I'd bought when I first adopted him. He'd never learned any tricks, but he had enough of his own. God, I loved that scroungy cat!

When Vito came out of the bathroom he was dressed in the corduroy suit. "Pants fit okay, a little loose in the waist but—well, how do I look?"

"Fine." He did, too. He'd washed up and combed his hair. He looked, actually, not much the worse for wear; there was about him something pulled together and trim. As I watched him put his shoes on, the thought occurred that he might be one of those who score A in Compulsive Survival.

He went about getting the rest of his things together. "You know what I been thinking? I never done anything right in my life, except maybe brush my teeth. I end up all fucked up. Why not? You, you're a whole different ball game. What happens? You end up equally screwed up. So—if that's the way the Old Lady pulls the strings, what's the use tryin'? Makes you think, don't it?"

I could see him pondering this as he collected his coat and put his gun into the airline bag. "Except that can't be it, know how I know? Ben would call that kind of rap a bummer. He wouldn't stand for down-heads. He was a great one for signs, like takin' a bummer and turning it into a sign to—like, change something, spin off in a different orbit. What do you think?"

"Me? I'm all thought out. Truth." I handed him the shopping bag and asked him to take it down with him

Vito looked inside. "Hey, don't throw this stuff out. I bet I could find another little kitty for you."

"I don't want a cat, I really don't like cats."

"You liked your cat—"

"I liked my cat, I loved *that* cat, but I don't particularly like cats in general."

"Okay, okay—what about a dog? I'll bet I could find you a cute little puppy?"

I laughed at his persistence. And I marveled at his endurance. "Why—you know of a pet shop you can knock off?"

"No, guy—come on. But I'd find you a puppy."

"Vito, I wouldn't want you snatching a puppy from some little old bowlegged blue-haired lady on Christopher Street."

The forehead wrinkled. "Hey, I wouldn't do anything like that. I'd like to do *something* for you. The main reason—your book. You don't know how bad I feel about that. Truth! Also, what the hell, you been good to me."

The straighter his line, the more I had to laugh. "*Good to you!*"

"Yeah. Oh, you started out sorta mean, but outside of that—well, listen, it wasn't boring."

I shook my head.

"No kidding. I could have done without"—now he gave me a small dig—"your freaky friends. Even that—well, it was vivid, if you know what I mean. So—" Vito stuck out his hand. "Happy New Year."

"Happy New Year."

"Oh, listen, I left you a few joints on the counter over there." He walked toward the door, turned around and hesitated before speaking. "Uh—can I call you or—drop by sometime? You know, just to say hello?"

"Sure."

He grinned. "I can?"

"Yeah, give me time to catch my breath."

"Well, so long. Good luck! I wish you good luck, guy."

"So long, Vito. Happy hunting."

I closed the door after him. I started to turn the bed down, but then I stopped and walked to the windows. The snow fell lightly, very lightly now. I was watching for Vito. There he came, crossing the street to the large trash can on the far side. He dropped the shopping bag in it. He began to walk away, down the street in thick snow halfway up to his knees. Then he suddenly stopped, turned around, looked up, and saw me. He waved. In that instant I had a flickering impulse to open the window and shout "What the hell—come on back!" I overcame it—what was his phrase?—ga-noog is ga-noog. I waved back and quickly stepped away from the window.

Within minutes I was in bed. There was only conscious time enough left to miss the warmth of Bobby Seale flattened out against my thigh and curse him for dying.

A phone call from the veterinarian awakened me the next day, New Year's. We quickly concluded funeral arrangements for Bobby Seale. It was not difficult to get back to sleep.

Next on the agenda, my agent, Phyllis. She'd been to a New Year's party. The word had gotten around about my job and this was the good news:

"Andreas Ffolkes was there, he's bringing one of those heavy costume plays over from England. When he heard about your bad luck—he's an old friend of mine—he gave me his word he'd find something for you in it. The principals are coming over from London, so there'll only be the smaller parts, soldiers, messengers, several young monks. It's a heavy production and they're only paying minimum, but it would be a job."

She was putting me right back to sleep. Phyllis picked up on my silence. "At least you'd be getting a weekly salary, Jimmy. Your unemployment's run out, hasn't it?"

"Yes."

"So look at it this way, it would help qualify you for next year. The deal is, you'll have to come by the theater in three or four weeks when they're casting and read for the director, but Andreas will be there and he said he'd *damn well see to it* you get something."

I used my grogginess as an excuse to end the conversation, telling Phyllis I'd call her in a day or so.

Under the heading Bright Prospects, this thirty-eight-year-old actor could look forward to a three- or four-week wait to audition for a bit part at minimum salary in an English import. I could hardly wait to be listed in the *Playbill* as "Soldiers, monks, virgins, bell-ringers—and humpbacks."

"No," I said out loud. "No hard feelings, but no!"

I was feeling hollowed out and wobbly from the last few days but still, at that very moment, I knew I would make a change. I took two more aspirin and went back to sleep.

It was the phone that awakened me again; Claire from the airport. Although it was late in the afternoon, it was still an effort for me to talk, especially to her. After telling me how terrible I sounded, she invited me once more to join her in Tobago. I declined again. "Jimmy, I know you're upset about—well, about things. Promise if there's anything I can do to help, you'll let me know. That's what family is for."

It hit me. By God, she'd asked and I would no longer criticize her for *my* silence. I'd level and see what it brought. I sat up in bed, cleared my throat, and asked if she had a minute to spare. She did.

"Claire, I want to get back to work on the book. I'm going to have to move. Instead of taking another apartment maybe I could find some little place up in the country for a winter rental or out West, where I could get away and really buckle down If you could lend me enough to get through the winter, I'd repay you when I go back to work, or if the book is published from anything I might make."

She pitched right in. "Jimmy, I've an idea and see if it isn't perfect? Why, I'm suddenly so excited. The market's down now and to raise cash I'd have to sell at a loss." (Not true, she kept large balances in both checking and savings accounts.) "But there's the house in Riverdale. You can have your own bedroom and the upstairs study all to yourself. You won't have to worry about cooking, or laundry or anything. You won't have to do anything but write your heart out. In the evening we can have a cocktail before dinner and you can tell me all about your day's work. I can even proofread for you. It's perfect, I've always wanted you to get more use out of that house. You can move up anytime. Jimmy, I'm so excited, what a lovely winter we'll have!"

I could not reply, the idea was disastrous. When I remained silent, she added: "It wouldn't cost you a cent, what do you say—is it a deal?"

"Claire, I honestly think it might be best if I just go someplace and hole up by myself."

"Any writer would give his right arm to have a setup like yours. That lovely house, everything taken care of, all the luxuries of home."

I decided to be entirely candid. "In other words, you won't lend me the money?"

"Jimmy, I explained, the market's down now and—"

"That's all I wanted to know."

A chilly pause before she said: "I'm amazed at your attitude, an offer like that—"

"Claire, I'm a grown man, can't you see if I'm plunging into work on something like this it might be best if I'm off by myself?"

"Jimmy, with all due respect, you might be a grown man, but if you're not able to support yourself—"

"Better not miss your plane. I'll see what I can work out. Have a good trip."

That ended the conversation and began my resolve: never to be dependent upon her again. She was a living Maypole; I would be forever entangled in the ribbons of her conditions unless I made a clean break.

Two resolutions taken care of! Oh, the relief. The relief of the *relief*! I didn't quite know how I'd manage, but I'd figure that out when I felt up to it. It was dark outside. I looked at the clock—almost five. Still feeling weak, I thought I'd better put something in my stomach, so I fixed some soup and made a light supper.

I came across Vito's cue card on the kitchen floor. While I ate, I looked it over. On the opposite side from the jokes and one-liners was printed *Real Life*. Underneath, written in his minuscule hand, were listed:

"Beetie's fucked-up parakeet, Marcy locked meat freezer, Marcy-me-tulips"—that one I knew—"Jitters—vibrator—St. V's Hosp, meet Judy Garland, fire-168th St. 5-times one night, dead body Jitters' car, Uncle S. pukes punchbowl, Maw-Paw-Toodles-Coney, EPS"—sic; ESP, I imagined—"with Lou & table knocking Hilda-witch, wino blows 9 in jail, Coby & Rita's prettiest wedding"—these two side-by-side items killed me—"Aunt L pee's Macy's, Richie's maid into brownies, BAD TRIP, Richie-me-Paris whore, Jitters' concussion, Hitching to S.F. with nut, Jitters'—snakes, movie star party, screwed-out-pay porno flick, Tijuana raid, spooky house Bev Hills, lady-pet cougar, Jitters & Sophia Loren, gay senator, sour cream—armpit, flat tire dessert [sic] all nite, Jitters' funeral."

I was sorry Jitters died. At least he seemed to have led a fairly eventful life.

The card was immeasurably touching.

Vito! Vito was certainly the most vivid character I'd encountered in many a year.

There was no contest over what to do with this New Year's Day—sleep it away. Back in bed I wondered what Vito was up to, how he was making out. Before falling asleep again, I wished him well, wished him a wide streak of good luck.

Kate woke me the following morning. Her curiosity had mushroomed, if anything. After commenting on my froggy tones, she struck right to the heart of her call. "Jim, now level with me. What was all the—"

"Kate, I still can't talk—" I croaked sleepily.

"It's almost eleven!"

I was being unduly mean but I couldn't stop myself. "We had a big night." I pulled my voice down to the barest whisper. "I can't talk now . . ."

"All right, you listen to me. I'm going to Washington, I'll be shooting there until the day after tomorrow, then I'm coming back and you and I are having dinner. I'm paying, *you're* talking! Good-bye!"

This started my day off in a good mood. I lay in bed laughing. Dear old Kate. I had a full morning erection. Dear old Kate, indeed. Because of our stormy holidays we had not been to bed since before Christmas. So, yes, there were thoughts of Kate.

I also thought of Vito. I wondered what that would have been like? Whatever, it probably would not have been boring.

Quickly I got out of bed and went into the bathroom to urinate. That would relieve some of the tension. While washing up I caught sight of myself in the mirror. I hadn't shaved for days; I looked scroungy. I liked the look and decided to keep it a while. I showered though and this made me feel fresher.

While eating breakfast, I once again looked over Vito's card. I don't know why it affected me so, but it did. Would he miss it, I wondered? Supposing he met a possible hook-up, would he be lost without it?

As I dawdled over coffee, what I should do now came to me in a series of calm overlaps. Mr. Weisscoff had said I could expect a settlement of fifteen hundred or two thousand if I vacated the premises early. I would move to a reasonable apartment and devote full time to writing the book. There would be no phone installed and I would tell Phyllis I would not be available for readings or interviews until I'd finished.

I had nine hundred rehearsal pay and the five hundred Claire had given me for Christmas. I also had bills amounting to over three hundred. I was not really flush. Perhaps I could get a part-time job that would bring in an extra fifty or sixty a week.

I would hole up, dig in, and write. Thirty-eight was old enough to start on a first novel without dragging it out, hit or miss, dabbled at and strung out and watered down by every possible interruption, physical and psychic. If I were going to give it a serious try, and I was, this was the approach, all or nothing.

Thoughts of the immediate future excited me. I'd made a Command Decision, by God. I phoned Mr. Weisscoff and told him to begin investigating a deal with the new owners.

Then, for something to do, I set to work to clean up the disaster area that was my apartment. By the time I finished, it was after three. Although the apartment was now back in order, it was somehow stale. Or I was stale in it. I needed to shop for food, needed fresh air more. Downstairs in the mailbox I found a New Year's card and Claire's check for two hundred and fifty dollars. It was appreciated; despite my resolves I was neither fool enough nor brave enough to send it back.

Walking through the snow, which had not yet turned to gray mush, I felt buoyant. The adrenaline of change stirred deep inside me. I shopped and bought a copy of the *Village Voice* in case there might be some advertisements for part-time jobs.

By the time I got home, the streak-ends of a mild pastel winter sunset were to be seen out my window over the rooftops to the west of me. I made myself a drink and toasted myself into the New Year on this second day of January. I picked up the *Voice* and, at the front of the paper, scanned the personal ads, which always fascinated me. "Gloria—come home, goldfish wilting, puppy won't eat, I can't sleep. Apologies. Sid." "Hey, Skinny, if you show up Friday night, I'll fatten you up. Love, Moo-Moo."

I made one up: "Vito, contact your former captor. For the main reason, you left your Personality Card. P.S. How goes it with you?"

The help-wanted ads were not nearly as much fun. Most of them sounded cold and impersonal. I had really never taken a regular job, so what did I know about them? What could I do? I sat there muddling. The future didn't loom quite as rosy as it had seemed earlier. The thought of working as maître d' or typist or waiter didn't fill me with anything like elation. The idea of apartment hunting was nothing to be looked forward to either; it would have to be small and fairly drab to fit my wallet.

To get down to fundamentals, my love affair with the city had begun to cool several years before. It was now kaput. The winters were no longer exciting, as they had been when I was twenty or thirty. (Exciting—had they ever been *exciting*? Yes.) I also remembered the good old days when the only knowledge one had of robberies and muggings was an occasional item in the *News* or *Mirror*. Now all you had to do for the latest reports was talk to a friend.

I shivered. I wasn't cold. I was, quite frankly—lonely. That's what I was, I was goddamn lonely! September, October, November, December, now January. I wondered how long the strength of missing Pete would grip me.

I missed Kate, too, although I knew only too well we'd reached the punishment phase of our relationship. Still, I missed the early months when round-the-clock infatuation—and novelty—made our time together so full of exuberance and warmth.

Bobby Seale, another hunk of warmth missing.

I was depressing myself. And doing a good job of it. I got up and wandered around the room. There on the kitchen counter were the joints Vito had left me. I picked one up. Why not? *Why not!*

I lit the joint and took a puff, holding it down only a few seconds before coughing the smoke back up. Vito would have awarded demerits. Taking another drag, I concentrated on holding, *holding* it down. Seven, eight, nine, ten—the heat of the smoke warmed my stomach.

"There . . ." I exhaled. I smoked again, contracting my stomach muscles, refusing to cough. Grinning at my expertise, I let the smoke out in a slow controlled stream.

After putting the original cast album of *Candide* on the stereo, I lay down on the bed and proceeded with Pot Smoking Two. Within a few minutes I felt a sort of cocked-hat calm settle over me. By the time I'd finished the joint and stubbed it out, my cares were dissolving to a surprising degree.

I did not usually have the happy built-in faculty of viewing the bumpy stretches as a series of jokes. Pete had always said, "Life is nothing but a bunch of revue sketches. The birth sketch, the first-day-at-school sketch, the discovering-what-your-dong-is-for sketch, the marriage one, and so on. Some are bombs, some are so-so, a few are perfect, but when they're played out—forget them. On to the next. And remember, like revue sketches, the bad ones always end."

So . . . ? No sweat, roll with 'em. They could not go on this way, that was for sure. They wouldn't dare.

My senses knocked for attention. I cocked my head. The music sounded, to my slightly stoned ears, as if the entire New York Philharmonic had dropped by for a visit. I glanced around the room. The texture of the exposed brick was astonishing to behold. The wall opposite the bed looked so alive it could have been breathing. Great Breathing Bricks! The apartment was friendly again, and I'd relaxed to the point of relative contentment. So long, spooks.

In a paean to pot, I wished I had smoked with Kate. I gave myself a few mental belts for having resisted. I don't know how long I lay there. After a while I got up to see if there was more ice cream in the freezer section. I didn't want it that second, but I wanted to know it was there. There was a pint of butter-almond. Joy!

There was also, nestled inside the cellophane packet, one other rolled cigarette. It was a bit the worse for wear, crumpled and slightly wilted. I straightened it out with loving care. So close to Heaven, why not make an entrance?

I switched the record to side two and aimed for the bed. I became aware of my movement; it was both light and heavy. Explain that, I thought. Well, as if I were in a weighted suit but light in the atmosphere. Like an astronaut? Who cares, both light and heavy!

Lighting up again, I took a deep drag. The stereo was tuned up high. Even so, I heard something, some other sound, or perhaps I only sensed . . . I glanced around the room. There was nothing. I listened. I did hear movement, muffled and—

I leaned back against the headboard of the bed and looked up above me. The small skylight, slightly to my left, joggled, moved slightly up, then back down on its rim, then swung up and away on its hinges. A drift of snow sprinkled down on the bed next to me.

I was not, I remember, alarmed. I believe I was more amused than anything.

A face appeared, Vito's face, grinning down at me. I would have grinned back immediately, but it was not exactly the same face I'd seen last. It was badly beaten—bruised forehead, black-eyed, swollen-jawed, and cut-lipped. Still, he grinned and then crossed his eyes. The crossed eyes did it; I couldn't help grinning back.

He uncrossed his eyes and spoke. "You probably don't remember me, but . . ."

I laughed at his line, but not at his face. "Vito! What happened to you!"

"Fuck it, I don't care!" He laughed again.

I had no idea what could be funny about his condition, but I was high so I laughed, too. "What are you doing up *there*, why didn't you knock on the front door?"

"I called you a little while ago, no answer."

"Oh, I was out for a while."

"So, I thought you wasn't home, figured I'd drop in and wait. I come over from the other roof." He thought for a moment. "Hey, if I had of knocked, would you let me in?"

"Sure."

"Can I come in now—I mean, down?"

"Does a bear shit in the woods?"

His head bobbed up and out of sight. When he reappeared, he

held a large canvas duffel bag over the skylight. I moved out of the way, and he let it fall to the bed, then dropped his airline bag down after it. "I got a bad ankle, maybe I better just come down from the roof. Let me in, huh?"

He shut the skylight and I walked, weaving slightly, to the front door and opened it. Vito came down the short flight of stairs from the roof and walked in, limping badly. Close up, he looked much worse. There was a lump on his jaw the size of a small walnut, the ridge on his forehead was raised and angry-looking, unhealthy yellows and reds edged the blue-black swelling of his bloodshot right eye.

"Jesus, Vito, when did *that* happen?"

He closed the door and locked it. "Other night, the bastards! Fuck 'em!" A hoarse laugh. "And I did." He sniffed the air, quickly took in the joint I was holding. "Hmn, good stuff, where'd you get it?"

"I grow it in old sweat socks."

He reached out; I handed it to him and he took a deep drag. Exhaling, he said: "So, how things been in the New Year?"

"Just as great as the old."

"Yeah? Tough . . ." He shrugged. "They picked up for me."

"You couldn't tell from looking at you."

"Looks isn't everything. Hey, could I have a glass of milk?"

"Sure, sit down." I got it for him and he sat on the bed. When he finished drinking, I held out the joint to him. "No, one puff's enough. I don't want to get high. Uh-uh." He screwed his face up to deadly earnest. "For the main reason—I want to make sense. I want to talk serious to you."

"Oh . . . ? Okay." I laughed. It was *for the main reason* and his attempt at solemnity that did it.

His forehead wrinkled. "What are you laughing for?"

"I'm a little high." The pot gave me the freedom to add: "Also, I'm—I feel very glad to see you again."

His face brightened and he grinned. "Yeah . . . ? Hey, how come you smoked—like all by yourself?"

"Seemed like a good idea."

"So, okay, what do you suppose is in there?" He patted the duffel bag.

"Search me. No, wait a minute, a cat? A kidnaped cat?"

"No—wrong."

"A puppy? A hot one—just snatched!"

Vito shook his head. "No—two wrong. Okay, wise-ass, you're shootin' for three wrong." A twinkle shone in his eyes, even the bloodshot one. "Pick a number between one and twelve."

"One and twelve?"

After a second he asked: "Got it?"

"Yeah."

"What is it?"

"Nine."

He spoke rapid-fire without taking a breath. "Wrong, *seven*, you lose, pull off your clothes and lie down!"

We both laughed. I sat down on the bed as Vito smacked his hands together. "I made more contacts with that one. If I seen a score, like a humpy number at a bar, I'd go up and cold, right off the bat: Think of a number between one and twelve. Five. Wrong, three, you lose, pull off your clothes and lie down! And you know what? It always broke the ice."

"You're an extremely vivid person."

"Vivid, yeah, you got that from me. Sometimes I think you put me on. Go ahead, put me on, I don't care. I got a question to ask you."

"Shoot."

"How long would it take you to write your book?"

"I don't know, ten months, eight months, a year. Why—do I have cancer?"

"Hey, guy, bite your tongue." He leaned forward and cracked his knuckles. "So—what about going away someplace?"

"Can't afford it."

"What if you could?"

"The way I feel today even Newark looks good." I held the butt out to Vito, who waved it away. "Except I have to admit, I'm beginning to feel better. This stuff sure picks a person's spirits up."

"I'm gonna pick 'em up even better. What about Mexico, could you live on eighty-six hundred for ten months or a year? Remember in Mexico, so it's cheaper by lots."

I thought a moment. "If I scrimped. I'd have to run my own tub, cut my own fingernails, but I could probably squeeze by."

Vito spoke with businesslike finality. "Well, if you can get by on that—you got a deal."

"Did I win the lottery?"

He stood up from the bed. "No, guy—you won *me!*"

I laughed. "Jesus, I knew my luck had run out for sure."

"Sticks and stones can break my bones, but insults don't mean dick!"

The amount I'd smoked was just now catching up with me. My head was stuffed with kapok, balloon-light and floating free. It suddenly struck me that—yes, Vito was back in the flesh, standing there in front of me, even though I couldn't comprehend what he was talking about. I shook my head, "Whew—this stuff is dynamite!"

"Wait'll you get a load of *this* stuff!" Vito opened his outer jacket, loosened his belt, and jammed a hand inside his pants, down into his crotch. When he pulled it out, he held a large wad of bills. He flipped off a rubber band and tossed the money on the bed next to me. "That's for starters, thirty-six hundred in cash. Half is yours."

"Mine?"

"Yeah, and that's only the first course." He leaned over the bed, opened the neck of the duffel bag, reached in, and pulled out a round metal cookie cannister, the gift type decorated with flowers. He lifted the top off, tilting it so I could see inside. "This, in here— pure cocaine, uncut. I'm gettin' five thousand for it tomorrow, nine thirty A.M. That's five and thirty-six, that's eight thousand six hundred—right?"

"Right."

Vito let out a high "Hee!" and said, "We hit it big, Jim-may! We're in the clover." I could only look at him with a certain amount of turned-on wonderment. "You wanna hear?"

"What do you think?"

"Okay, I'm gonna tell you." Forgetting about his ankle, he executed a little jump step in the air. He winced. "Oh, shit—oew!"

"Vito, what about your face, isn't there something—"

"Naw, I already been to the emergency. They give me the treatment, all it takes now is for it to heal. I'm okay, honest. So, get this, I had this friend, Jitters, my best friend, and—"

"Oh, you left your card here."

"Yeah, I figured. Anyhow, Jitters was—well, he was the most vivid character ever. Oh, no sex, we was just best friends. Crazy he was, but, oh, what a kick! And funny! Time to time he used to be a runner for different deals, hash, smack, different stuff. Me and Jitters, too, used to run for this guy, Joe Bistrante, oh, big hot-shot dresser but strictly minor Mafia. Joey Bistrante sent Jitters to Harlem on a strictly bad deal two years ago, before I went to the coast with Ben. Sent him right into a den of crazies. Jitters got stabbed to death by this strung-out spade nut.

"Jitters didn't have no family so a bunch of us chipped in, everybody loved Jitters, and we gave him a sendoff would knock your eyes out. Joey Bistrante blah-blah'ed out of the funeral expenses but he promises to buy Jitters a good stone, you know, for his grave. It's now almost two years and I ain't seen no stone, did you? Uh-uh.

"Okay, get this." Vito cracked his knuckles and backed off a few steps. Legs planted apart, cocky of stance, he took the floor as if he were taking stage. "So, the writer here"—he jabbed a thumb at me—"the writer here has to be alone. Mr. Big Thinker gotta have his solitude, so I'm out on my ass in the snow. Right? Right. After

I hit the streets, I stopped off at an all-night diner. I was fuckin' starvin'! Ow, you should have seen what I put away. I mean it, Jimmy, I was gettin' laughs from the waitress.

"Then I stopped off at this private club on the West Side I know, run by the gang. Maybe I can latch on to a little deal. Who's there but Joey Bistrante and his wife, Ella, the both of them dressed to the teeth. I get a drink and they wave, so I go over and sit and we blah-blah-blah real chummy. So chummy that I finally say, 'Hey, Joey, what about Jitters' stone? It's goin' on two years now.' I said it real nice cause he promised and it burns my ass that Jitters is out in Queens now two years with no marker, nothin'.

" 'Yeah, I gotta take care of that,' Joey says. When, I ask, is all I ask, is when. And his wife, Ella, suddenly pipes up. 'Oh, stop bugging him about Jitters for Chrissake, it's New Year's.' 'Hey, wait a minute,' I says, 'it's New Year's out at Queen of Angels Cemetery, too, and Jitters ain't got—'

" 'Oh, go fuck your stupid self!' Ella says. Joey gets a big kick, almost falls off his chair, out of his wife saying this big clever line *go fuck your stupid self!* Oh, how he laughs, you'd think she'd just quoted Shakespeare outta the mouth of Lenny Bruce. And when he finally pulls himself together, he says, yeah, come to think of it, that's what I should do—go fuck myself. Then Ella—mind you they're oiled, but still, for a woman to talk like that! Ella says, 'Yeah, and while you're at it, why don't you dig up your friend Jitters and go fuck him, too!' "

Vito stopped and stared at me. "You ever hear of such a filthy dirty thing to say about someone dead, someone that you caused to be dead? I couldn't believe my ears, especially from a good-lookin' woman all dressed up for New Year's.

"Now Joey Bistrante is *hysterical*, it's so funny. I was shocked, I was so shocked I says to Ella, 'Why you stupid fuckin' sacrilegious *cunt*, you!' And the fight was on. Joey and one of the club goons dragged me outside. And Ella, she comes out on the sidewalk, takes off her shoe, and gives me this with the heel." Vito pointed to the bruise on his forehead.

He held up a warning hand. "Oh, baby, that really did it, that *did* it! Last night I waited across from their building, brownstone over in Murray Hill, and sure enough about seven thirty out they come, all dolled up again, Ella lookin' like a million. But the mouth on her!

"Now, I'll tell you, I mainly thought if I get enough for a good stone, like a nice angel, that would be it. I figured whatever hockables would do it. But once inside I kept remembering how vulgar they was and I said to myself—they're gonna pay for it. I went crazy. I tore that apartment apart from the seams and I don't usually do that. Wasn't I neat with you? Just took the stuff, no mess, huh?"

I nodded and grinned. I was rooting for him, even though I knew the results.

"You know what I got special fun out of—ripping *her* off for the foul mouth on her. Truth, Jimmy, the majority of the thirty-six hundred came from her stuff, her jewelry, which she had a lot of, and two good fur coats. I took his jewelry, too, and some other stuff. Now, it's not until I'm practically leaving that I remember to check inside the toilet."

"Inside the toilet?"

"Yeah, about three years ago when I went to his apartment to pick up some stuff for delivery, I remembered he got it out of the toilet tank, the top part where you keep the water for the flush. So, I go to the john and I lift off the lid and—there's the cookie can all sealed, watertight. I nearly shit, I was so excited. Oh, Jimmy, I shouted for joy!"

Vito laughed and slapped a hand against his chest. "You know what I did before I left—I mean they would figure out it was me anyhow—so I took one of Ella's lipsticks and wrote on their bedroom mirror: *J I T T E R S   W A S   H E R E!*

"Jitters was here!" he repeated, clapping his hands together. "Can you see their *faces*?" He had a solid laugh at that prospect.

"I picked out an angel for Jitters today. I seen several big ones but they looked mean as hell, scowling angels. I finally found *one* that was smiling, a nice medium-sized happy-looking angel, cost $483, inscribed and everything. I got over four thousand for the hockables, but I spent that, which left thirty-six hundred."

Vito spoke with pride. "That's the biggest hit I ever made. Of course, the coke made it a winner. So, you see, Jimmy, I gotta go to Mexico or someplace 'cause if I stick around here, my ass out on the streets won't be worth three cents of bad dog meat. This is the way it looks to me, eighty-six hundred split is forty-three hundred apiece, so—"

"Split? Listen, Vito—"

"Ah-ah, half is yours." I began to speak but Vito raised his voice to a shout. "Jimmy, I know what I gotta do, goddamn it! I threw your fuckin' book out, that's the lowest! Jesus, let me have my pride back!" He spoke with such resolve that I sat there quietly. "Like I said, now forty-three hundred isn't a helluva lot for one, but eighty-six hundred stretches a lot longer for *two* living in Mexico. That's only one rent, food for two's not much more than food for one, one car for two and so on. Way I look at it we could—"

"Vito, I—"

"Will you listen to me out, what I got in my mind? I snag us some wheels, I can get a hot car, safe and cheap, and we light out for Mexico. We rent a pad, someplace where we like. You write your book and I resume my course on how not to end up a dumb schmuck at forty." I began to speak again. "Ah, ah, I do the shopping, fix the eats, keep the place all douched up spick-and-span—everything. All you gotta do is fly your fingers over the keys, spin the tales. So—what do you think?"

He was, actually, tickling the hell out of me. He was also astounding me, disarming me, *touching* me. And because of the way he was reaching me, I naturally had to punch the caution button. "Vito, the whole idea's wild!"

The shoulders hunched up, the hands went out in a gesture of supplication. "So—what do you want, to grab hold of a *dull* one?"

"No, but—" I had to laugh at him, with him, because of him. I shook my head. "Do you really see us as a winning team?"

Now his challenge, wise and tough: "Yeah—why in the fuck not? What's to win, anyway? You can split anytime you want. Winning team? What's that? We already won, we got the bread—bammo, just like that!" A thought struck him. "Oh, Jesus—you're not worried about *puttin' out*, are you? If that's what—"

"No, I wasn't even thinking about that."

"I'll bet. Listen, don't get 'em in an uproar. Sure, I'd like to toss the salad with you, but—if I get into your knickers, *you'll* do the unzipping. That's in a way of speakin'. *I* bet that's what's buggin' you. You know something, I may be a dumb-head but sometimes you're a dumb-*ass*. You get my point?"

"I think so," I grinned.

"One other thing, you think I'm doing this for *you*? Think again. I'm gonna level with you. Do me the favor to listen."

Instead of talking, he opened his airline bag, foraged around, and took out a dog-eared notebook; from it he took two wrinkled sheets of yellow paper. "Here." He handed them to me. One had a list of perhaps one hundred books, the other a long list of classical records. "That's Ben's handwriting, lists for my reading and listening education." He took them, carefully folded them up, and put them back in the notebook.

Then he faced me. "I am frantic to dummy up, Jimmy. Truth. I am A-Number-One Fuckin' Tired of being this world's dumb-head. I'll tell you something else—I don't even think it's *funny* any more!"

He walked to the mirror and looked at himself. "Look at me, you think I want to go through life getting the shit kicked out of me, makin' runs for the minor Mafia, their delivery boy? You think I like to hang out in bars so I can score, so maybe I can hook up with someone who'll feed me, let me sleep at their place? I told you I was twenty-seven. I'm thirty-fuckin'-one, nine years from four-oh. And look at me!"

He made a small gesture of disgust, then he opened the notebook and pawed through the pages until he found what he wanted. "Listen to what Ben said once. 'You better find out what you want in life, *because that's what you're going to get!*'

"Well, *I don't want what I had.* That's for sure. I want sometime to have my own house, my own job, my own car, my own wife, and my own kid. But mostly, my own pride in just being a person can mix with other people without puttin' on a freak show. I been a freak act and I want out of the sideshow." He thought a moment, then snorted and added: "And into the *main tent.*" A bronchial laugh. "Hey, that ain't bad, huh? I want out of the freak show and into the main tent."

"No, it's not."

"So . . . what do you say?"

"Vito, it's"—I was struggling against the effects of the marijuana; I realized I was in a weakened condition and had every reason to put up a fight—"it's—it's just too wild!"

"Wild? Wild for a writer, that should be good. Who says wild isn't good? Wild is great!" Vito snapped his fingers, took a little jump step and, despite his bad ankle, landed with his feet planted apart, toes turned out. He looked like a young Italian Cagney, about to go into his dance. "Okay—wild, wild? Flying—ey, what about that for wild? Who ever thought of *that* to begin with? What if that one brother—what's-his-face?"

"The Wright brothers, Wilbur and Orville."

"*Wilbur and Orville,*" he said, in a derisive voice. "Sound like a couple of tired old queens. So what if Wilbur had said to Orville: 'Fly—up in the air? Are you buggy, Mae?'

"Wild things is good. Pot is wild. What?—a couple of little puffs and you're in never-never land. And they say the Old Lady put everything on this earth Herself, every little plant and twig down to the ittiest bittiest gnat. So, She knew what She was doin'. She planted Maryjane. And—ah—*wild!* Yeah, that's my point."

He stopped, stood dead still for a moment, then snapped his

fingers. The expression on his face announced he had a big one. "Okay, look at Grace Kelly!"

"*Grace Kelly?*"

"Yeah, Grace Kelly. Started out a poor little pussy from Pittsburgh—"

"Philadelphia."

"Philadelphia—Pittsburgh, big deal!"

"And she was rich to begin with."

"Okay, still a little pussy from Philadelphia and now she's a goddamn *Princess!*"

"She was already a big fat movie star!"

Vito dismissed Grace Kelly with a wave of his hand. "All right, all right—forget Grace Kelly! When I was a kid, I used to want to shtupp her. That's how she got in there. Anyhow, what do you say?"

"Vito, I can't make sense out of it. It doesn't—of course, I'm feeling a little woozy. *Good* woozy, but—"

He dug in his bag and took out another joint. "Not woozy *enough.* The whole thing set up, I knew you'd down-head me." He lit up, smoked, and exhaled. "Heavy! Klump-klump—you're heavy. The ballbreaker was right. You won't ever—what'd she say? Shake it up! You got lead shoes on. Not only that, you got your feet stuck in glue. Old glue-shoes."

"Up yours!"

He flashed a wide frozen grin. "Okay!" Then snapped it shut again.

I reached for the cigarette. He held it back. "Better not, you won't be able to make *sense* out of—whatever it is you gotta make sense out of." I took it from him and smoked. "You know what you are? You're a *senso* freak!" Vito giggled. "And remember, this offer expires at midnight—1999. In New Jersey the number is Bigelow blah-blah-blah-blah-blah-blah—"

I chipped in with him to sound the raspberry, then we laughed.

"What a vivid New Year's!" I said. I took another puff and thought about Pete, wondering if he could see me now.

Do they get to peek at us?

I felt a definite tilt. But better than the tilt, I was beginning to feel—loose. Yes, loose and free.

Pete, look who's loosening up! I know what you'd say, which way you'd push. Pete, who had once said, "The greatest thing in life, almost as good as sex, but a helluva lot longer lasting—is friendship! Friendships—Jesus, what would we do without them?"

Yes, and I thought: oh, the varying sizes, shapes, and qualities of them. Not always, but sometimes—they come along just when we need them.

Do we take them where we find them? Or do we throw them back?

"Hey . . ." Vito's hand reached out.

I handed the joint to this—friendship.

"You know what, you oughta start lookin' at things positively," Vito said. A brief bark of laughter. "So—what?—you had any *better* offers today?"

He had a way of getting at the basics. I certainly hadn't; I'd been feeling low and lonely. I watched him while he smoked. The similarity between Bobby Seale and Vito hit me again. Only if I took on this cat, he would require more responsibility of me than just opening a can of tuna and a game of hide and seek now and then.

I glanced at his duffel bag, the money on the bed, the cookie cannister. Like any good cat he'd dragged his catch back to his chosen home.

I felt a great womping surge of warmth for him. I wanted to reach out and touch him.

Vito looked up at me. "What?" he asked. "A penny?"

By far the safest thing to pin it on was—"Umm, this stuff is glorious! Oh, Senegalese Thunderfuck, I love you!"

I wanted to pat him, to thank him for his gesture. I wondered how long I would go on pretending I had no arms.

Out of nowhere, I was struck by a burst of energy and a massive shot of general euphoria. I stood up on the bed. Vito had had his turn; I wanted mine. He sensed this, because he grinned, backed away, and sat down on a hassock. "Yeah?" he asked. "So—splat it out."

"I wonder, *does everything have to make sense?* I wonder. Even in the real world, as opposed to *now,* even when things *make* sense, they really don't make *sense.* Do they?"

Vito shrugged and giggled. "I pass, you're the sense freak."

"Okay, you finally get a break and before rehearsals even start, the star's boy friend gets fired in Spain for calling the director 'a dizzy cunt.' So, you, minding your own business way the other side of the *Atlantic,* get it—zap, in the neck! That doesn't make sense."

Vito handed me the joint. "Keep up the old steam, put it through the computer!"

I only had time for the quickest puff. "By Christmas I figured I got the world by the tail. I got a lead on Broadway, a girl to make great Hugglebunnyburgers with, I'm moving up, got my eye on the sparrow—then, zappo! By New Year's Eve, the Old Lady Up There, She pulls the rug out from under me. The whole rug, not just a corner. Whoosht—now you see it, now you don't! Right?"

"Right, tell me about it, lay it out for me!"

"Bammo, fired! No job. Then—wop! Eighty-six the girl and the H-B-burgers. Then, as if the Old Gal hadn't totaled me, I find a horny little wop burglar—wop again, no pun intended—under the *bed*. And I've already been cleaned out twice. Now that doesn't make a bit of sense!"

"Yeah," Vito said, "but that's what we're here for. Hit me with the *sense* of it. It gotta make *sense!*"

Now I was laughing, nice tumbling rolls of easy laughter. I held my arms out from my sides. For a moment I considered levitating. I turned to Vito. "No, no sense at all! So, get this, first I put his lights out, then I tie him up and figure to get him—what?— shtupped for New Year's. And who ends up almost getting it, no one but good old square-ass *me!* Now, really, you don't believe that!"

Vito Uncle Tommed me, rolling eyes and all. "I don't believes yah, but Ah hears yah talkin'.'"

"Pow! I fall into the world of pot and burglars and degeneracy and—bingo, before I can even start *maintaining* it, the little wop burglar bounces back forty-eight hours later with a load of goodies, a *dowry*, and—and an offer of marriage!"

Vito stamped his feet and shook his head. "I don't believe it, it don't make sense!" He broke off, laughing.

I was delighted with his delight.

"You know," Vito said, "you're not bad at all, once you get a head of steam up—and that's it, the whole schmeer?"

"What do you want for a nickel? Yes. And—no! Jesus, I forgot. Get this, there's a tag, a postscript. For the main reason—P.S., on top of it all, my *cat* is dead!"

Vito slapped the palm of his hand to his forehead. "Your *cat is dead*! Un-uh, that don't make a bit of sense!"

But suddenly it did. It was the wipe-out, the finish to an era, a period, the last tie broken. It was magically see-through-clear.

"Ah," I told him, "but it does, it *does!*"

Vito snapped his head around in a double-take. "It does?"

"Yes."

"Well, I'll be all powdered down in a star-spangled jockstrap! So, hit me with the wrap-up!"

"My pleasure. Now, get this, his *death*, the idea that he could walk out on me after the lavish display of Friskies and catnip, toys and scratching pads and assorted collars, jeweled and otherwise, and gourmet kitty food—flounder on Saturdays, fresh shrimp on holidays—that he could walk out on all I'd squandered on him, to say nothing of my love and affection, my heart, my very *heart*, that he would have the effrontery to do this to me, so enrages me, that I forsake the very land of my birth, the United States of America— and move to Mexico!"

I took a lovely free fall, the way trapeze artists leave their rigs for the net, and dropped to the bed in a sitting position. I bounced up and down in the pure freedom I was *allowing* myself. Yes, I could allow myself the indulgence of my emotions. Oh, the joy of it! And the release. Kabam, it hit me hard and big—as if all the planets and stars suddenly swung into the right position and my sign had an orgasm.

"Hey, Vito—Jesus, thank you!"

The phone rang.

As Vito dived onto the bed next to me I thought: I can laugh as long as you can ring.

And I did.

P.S.
And this is the book I wrote.

JAMES ZOOLE
Puerta Blanca
Mexico